CONTENTS

Rupert and the Pharaoh's Treasure.... 6

Rupert and the Star Gazer......... 26

Rupert and Odmedod's Adventure ... 46

Rupert and the Noisy Firework..... 66

Rupert's Anniversary Colouring
Competition.................... 81

Rupert Fun Pages............. 83

Rupert and the Christmas Tree..... 98

This book belongs to:

....

....

John Harrold.

Stories by **IAN ROBINSON**   Illustrated by **JOHN HARROLD**   Story colouring by GINA HART
The Publishers would like to thank The Followers of Rupert for their cooperation and assistance in selecting the Fun Pages

RUPERT

John Harold.

THE DAILY EXPRESS ANNUAL

Pedigree®
BOOKS

No. 60

Published by Pedigree Books Limited
The Old Rectory, Matford Lane, Exeter, EX2 4PS.

$13.99
RU60

RUPERT and the

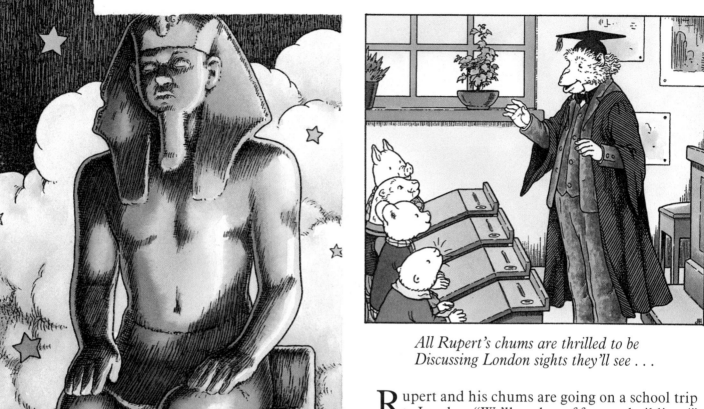

All Rupert's chums are thrilled to be Discussing London sights they'll see . . .

Rupert and his chums are going on a school trip to London. "We'll see lots of famous buildings!" says Dr. Chimp. "Let's see how many you can think of . . ." "There's the Houses of Parliament," says Rupert. "And St. Paul's!" cries Gregory. "I'd like to see the Tower of London," adds Ottoline. "I expect we'll see all those," chuckles Dr. Chimp. "We'll visit some interesting museums too. Don't be late! The coach leaves at eight o'clock sharp . . ."

Pharaoh's Treasure

"Remember, now! Please don't be late.
Our coach will leave from here at eight!"

Next morning Rupert's soon awake
And packs some sandwiches to take.

Next morning, after breakfast, Rupert's mother gives him some sandwiches to put in his satchel and tells him to run along, so he'll be in plenty of time to catch the coach. As Rupert arrives, he meets his pal, Bingo, hurrying towards the school gates. "Hello!" calls the brainy pup. "This should be a marvellous outing!" "Yes," says Rupert. "There are so many different things I want to see . . ."

He runs to school, and on the way
Meets Bingo, keen to start the day . . .

RUPERT GOES TO LONDON

The pals both laugh at Podgy, who
Has brought lunch – and a few snacks too!

"Good!" Dr. Chimp says. "Everyone
Is here on time. Our trip's begun!"

The coach arrives in London, then
A clock begins to strike – Big Ben!

The coach stops. "This Museum's where
We'll start our tour. Let's see what's there . . ."

Although it's early in the morning, Rupert soon spots more of his chums hurrying towards the coach, including Podgy Pig, who turns up carrying a huge hamper full of food! "It's a long way to London," he explains. "I thought I'd pack some elevenses too . . ." Dr. Chimp ticks off each of the pals' names as they climb aboard the coach and finally declares that everyone's arrived. "Time we were underway!" he cries as the driver starts his engine. "Next stop, London!" smiles Rupert.

Trundling along the country lanes that surround Nutwood, the coach finally reaches the main road to London . . . . "Keep your eyes open, now!" calls Dr. Chimp. "We should soon see some famous landmarks." "We're crossing the River Thames!" cries Ottoline excitedly. "Look!" says Rupert. "There are the Houses of Parliament!" When the coach stops, Dr. Chimp tells the chums they've arrived at the British Museum. "Let's go inside," he says. "There's an exhibition I want you all to see . . ."

"These statues are all kings, we know,
Called Pharaohs, who ruled long ago . . ."

"The Pharaoh's Gold!" says Ottoline
And points towards a sign she's seen.

Inside the room's a rich array
Of golden jewellery on display.

"The Pharaoh's necklace! Goodness me!
It's been here for a century!"

Following Dr. Chimp into the museum, Rupert finds himself in a great hall full of colossal statues. "These are all from Ancient Egypt," explains his teacher. "Some are almost four thousand years old!" "They look a bit stern!" says Gregory. "That's probably because they were Kings!" chuckles Dr. Chimp. "Pharaohs to be precise . . ." "Look at this!" cries Ottoline. "There's an exhibition of treasure!" "Yes," says Dr. Chimp. "It was all found in a single pyramid . . ."

As the pals enter the exhibition room they see case after case of gleaming gold objects. "What beautiful jewellery!" gasps Ottoline. In the middle of the room is a magnificent necklace, set in a special showcase. "It was worn by the Pharaoh himself," reads Ottoline. "The wealthiest ruler Egypt had ever seen. His treasure was discovered by someone digging near the pyramid a hundred years ago. He gave it to the museum to put on display and it's been here ever since . . ."

9

RUPERT SEES THE SCIENCE MUSEUM

"Come on!" calls Bingo. "Time we went!
I'd rather see things folk invent!"

"This way!" says Dr. Chimp. "Our tour
Has fascinating treats in store . . ."

"Inventions and machines that go
Are what this building has to show."

The wheels and cogs begin to spin.
"Gosh!" Ottoline gasps. "What a din!"

Rupert and Ottoline are still marvelling at the Pharaoh's treasure when Bingo announces their next destination . . . "Jewellery and statues are all very well, but wait till you see the Science Museum! It's full of wonderful engines and inventions." "You can make some of them work, can't you?" asks Rupert. "That's right!" says Bingo. "All you do is press a button . . ." A few minutes later, Dr. Chimp assembles the whole group and leads them back to the coach.

When the chums reach the Science Museum, Rupert can soon see why Bingo was so keen to come. Everywhere he looks there are devices and inventions, each of which seems bigger and more complicated than the last. "Watch carefully," says Dr. Chimp. He presses a button and a machine clatters into life. "These were used in old factories," he explains. "They were the first of their kind ever made . . ." "Noisy contraptions!" sniffs Ottoline. "I'd rather see more statues!"

RUPERT DISAPPEARS

The pals look for machines to try.
"This one seems tucked away, but why?"

The three pals are convinced that they
Have found a sort of motor sleigh.

Then Rupert suddenly spins round
To see a lever Bingo's found.

"Come back!" his chums cry in dismay
As Rupert slowly fades away . . .

Dr. Chimp tells the chums they can go off and explore on their own. Bingo decides to show Rupert his favourite machine, but spots something even more interesting, hidden away in a dusty corner. "What's that?" asks Ottoline. "I don't know," says Bingo. "Let's take a closer look . . ." "Perhaps it's a mechanical sledge?" says Rupert. "There's a seat here, and some levers to work the controls." "What a find!" says Bingo excitedly. "I can just imagine it, skimming over the frozen snow . . ."

Rupert is still sitting at the control panel when Bingo spots another lever down behind the seat. "I wonder what that's for?" he asks. Rupert spins round to look and accidentally knocks something with his elbow. All at once a low hum starts to echo round the room. "W . . . what's happening?" gasps Ottoline. "Push the lever back!" calls Bingo, but it is too late . . . To the chums' astonishment, Rupert and the strange machine get fainter and fainter, then completely disappear!

RUPERT TRAVELS THROUGH TIME

The strange machine appears to fly
Through banks of thick cloud in the sky.

It jolts and Rupert starts to fall.
He lands outside, but that's not all . . .

"What's happened?" Rupert blinks. "Why, I'm
Convinced I've travelled back in time!"

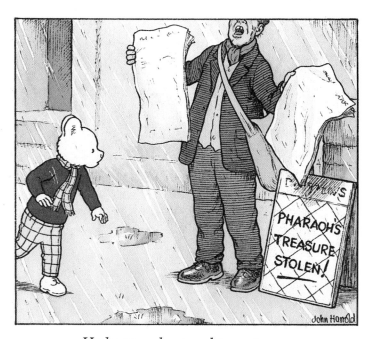

He hears a shout and turns to see
A sign, "Museum Robbery!"

"Push the lever back . . ." Rupert hears Bingo's call, but, as he leans forward, everything starts to spin round and round. His chums vanish, the room fades and thick banks of cloud scud past at tremendous speed. "I . . . I'm flying!" cries Rupert as the machine jolts violently from side to side. The next moment, he topples out of the seat and tumbles slowly through the clouds, landing with a gentle bump on a smooth, hard surface. "Where am I?" he gasps. "What's happened to the museum?"

As Rupert clambers to his feet, he can hardly believe his eyes! There are horse-drawn carriages clattering along the street and everywhere he looks he sees people in old-fashioned clothes, hurrying to get out of the rain. "I must have travelled back in time!" he gasps. "Museum robbery!" comes a nearby cry. "Read all about it!" Rupert spins round and sees a sign declaring the Pharaoh's Treasure has been stolen. "How odd," he blinks. "The display we saw this morning!"

RUPERT MEETS A NEW FRIEND

A carriage stops to hear the shout
Then drives off as a man gets out.

He doesn't notice Rupert there
And bumps into the little bear . . .

"So sorry! All my fault. I say!
You'd better get dry straightaway . . ."

"It's lucky that I live so near!
I'll tell my housekeeper you're here . . ."

Rupert is still gazing in amazement at his surroundings, when a man in a bowler hat hops out of a cab and hurries across the road to buy a paper. Although it's still raining, he opens it immediately and starts to read as he walks along. " 'Pon my soul!" he cries. "The thing's impossible!" He is so busy reading that he doesn't notice Rupert and bumps into him, sending him flying. Before he can save himself, Rupert is bowled over and lands in a cold, deep puddle . . .

"Goodness!" cries the stranger. "I do beg your pardon! All my fault. Should have been looking where I was going!" He helps Rupert to his feet, then apologises again for being so clumsy. "Don't worry," says Rupert. "I only got a bit wet." "A bit!" cries the man. "You're soaked through! Luckily, I live nearby. My housekeeper can dry your things before you catch a nasty cold. Come in," he says as they reach his house. "I'll let Mrs. Hudson know you're here . . ."

RUPERT HEARS AN ODD TALE

*"My name's John Watson. Have some tea.
You're welcome to stay here with me . . ."*

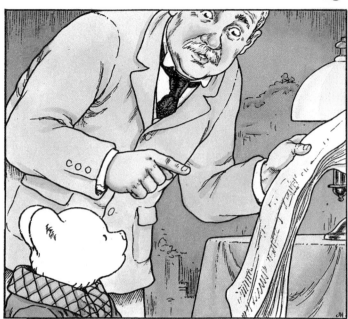

*"This Pharaoh Case! There's not a clue!
Though Holmes would soon know what to do!"*

*"Not Sherlock Holmes?" cries Rupert. "The
Most famous sleuth in history!"*

*"The same! But sadly, he's away,
Upon a lengthy holiday."*

No sooner has Rupert stepped through the door than a kindly old lady bustles out to greet him. "Soaked to the skin!" she tuts as she sees the state of his clothes. "We'd better wrap you in one of the Master's dressing gowns . . ." A few minutes later, Rupert is sitting by the fireside, drinking a cup of tea. "My name's John Watson," says the man. "I'm sorry to bump into you like that, but this Pharaoh business has got me baffled. If only Holmes were here. He'd soon know what to do . . ."

"Holmes?" cries Rupert. "Not Sherlock Holmes, the famous detective!" "The very same," smiles Watson. "Now, if *he* were here, the treasure would be found in no time. As it is, he's away on holiday and Scotland Yard have asked me to help solve the crime . . ." "How did it happen?" asks Rupert. "That's the problem," sighs Watson. "Nobody seems to know. The exhibition's been under strict police guard, but when the museum opened this morning, the Pharaoh's necklace had simply vanished."

RUPERT IS SURPRISED

When Rupert's clothes dry, Watson asks
If he would help him with some tasks . . .

"The first thing that we have to find
Are hidden clues of any kind!"

"This way!" says Watson, unaware
That Rupert's already been there . . .

Then Rupert cries out in surprise,
Unable to believe his eyes!

As soon as Rupert's clothes are dry, Dr. Watson says he's going to go and examine the scene of the crime. "Perhaps you'd like to come too?" he asks. "Two sets of eyes are always better than one. You might spot something I don't see!" Hailing a cab in the street outside, Watson gives the cabbie the address and the pair are soon speeding towards the British Museum, through the crowded streets of London. They arrive at the main entrance and hurry up the steps towards the door . . .

Inside the museum, Rupert recognises some of the statues he saw on the school outing . . . "The exhibition room's closed to the public, but the police are expecting me," explains Watson, as they make their way through the crowd of sightseers towards the Pharaoh's Treasure. "Scotland Yard assure me they've put one of their best men on the case," he adds, but, as they near the exhibition, Rupert stops suddenly and gives a cry of surprise. "It can't be!" he gasps.

RUPERT MEETS SERGEANT GROWLER

"It's P.C. Growler!" Rupert blinks.
"But how can he be here?" he thinks.

"Meet Sergeant Growler!" Watson beams.
Just a coincidence, it seems . . .

Inside the exhibition hall
A young policeman greets them all.

"He saw nobody come or go.
The necklace vanished, even so!"

"P.C. Growler!" cries Rupert, as he sees the policeman standing on duty outside the exhibition. "You know him?" asks Watson. "But this is *Sergeant* Growler. Holmes and I worked with him on an important case last year. A young assistant of mine," he says, introducing Rupert to the smiling policeman. "You look just like somebody I know in Nutwood," says Rupert. "He's a policeman too . . ." "Really?" chuckles the sergeant. "That's quite a coincidence!"

Inside the exhibition room, stands a second policeman, a young constable, called Timkins, who was on duty the night the robbery happened. "The Pharaoh's necklace was displayed here . . ." says Growler, pointing to an empty stand in the middle of the exhibits. "Hundreds of visitors came to see the treasure during the day, but the necklace was *still* here last night, after they'd all left. Timkins stayed on guard duty all evening, but when he made his rounds this morning it had vanished!"

RUPERT HAS AN IDEA

The case is simple, Watson thinks.
He's sure Timkins took forty winks!

But Rupert knows the treasure's bound
To be returned. "It must be found!"

"Come on!" says Watson. "Time for tea!
A sneak thief stole the jewellery!"

"No!" Rupert smiles. "I think you'll find
The necklace has been left behind!"

"I'm afraid there's only one explanation," declares Dr. Watson. "Young Timkins here must have nodded off and the thief took the necklace while he was asleep . . ." "No, sir!" cries Timkins. "I was wide awake all night!" "It's a regular mystery!" mutters Sergeant Growler. "Don't worry, I'm sure the necklace will be recovered," says Rupert. "It must be," he thinks to himself. "Ottoline and I saw it, back in place, years after the robbery is meant to have happened . . ."

Deciding that there is nothing more to be learned at the museum, Dr. Watson leads the way outside and hails a passing cab. "It's a shame about Timkins!" he sighs as they travel back to Baker Street. "He *must* have nodded off, though he seems certain no one got past him all night . . ." Rupert looks thoughtful, then gives a sudden cry. "Of course! If nobody left the room, then the necklace must still be there . . ." "But that's impossible!" splutters Watson. "You saw the empty display stand!"

RUPERT WAITS UNTIL IT'S DARK

When they reach Baker Street again
Rupert slips into Holmes's den . . .

He asks Watson to pack a light.
"We're going out again, tonight!"

As darkness falls, the pair return
To see what more there is to learn . . .

They reach the building silently,
Then break in with a special key.

As soon as they reach Baker Street, Rupert asks if he can borrow something from Holmes's laboratory. "Of course," says Dr. Watson. "But you still haven't told me what's happened to the missing necklace!" "Don't worry," smiles Rupert. "I'm sure it's safe and sound, but we'll have to wait until this evening to make certain . . ." "This evening?" gasps Watson. "Yes," says Rupert. "I'd like you to pack a set of keys and a small lantern. We're going back for a second look . . ."

When darkness falls, Rupert and Dr. Watson approach the museum on foot to avoid being noticed . . . The building is completely deserted as they tip-toe round to a side entrance and try the lock with a skeleton key. "This is all highly irregular," mutters Dr. Watson. "Anyone would think we were trying to rob the museum, rather than recover one of its treasures!" "It's the only way my plan will work," whispers Rupert. The door swings open and the pair slip stealthily inside.

18

RUPERT AND WATSON ARE STARTLED

Inside the main hall statues loom
As Rupert tip-toes through the gloom.

Then, suddenly, a dazzling ray
Of light shines and a voice calls, "Stay!"

It's Sergeant Growler! "I see you
Suspect the thief is still here too . . ."

"Shhh!" Rupert hisses. "Not a word.
We don't want to be overheard!"

Inside the museum, all is quiet as Rupert and Dr. Watson make their way towards the Pharaoh's Treasure . . . Rupert can see huge figures looming in the darkness and has a strange feeling he's being watched. "Nonsense!" chuckles Dr. Watson. "It's just your imagination. There's nobody here except statues!" As the pair reach the exhibition room they are suddenly dazzled by the glare of a powerful lantern. "Stay where you are!" orders a burly figure, stepping out from the shadows . . .

"It's Sergeant Growler!" gasps Dr. Watson. "Evening, sir," says the policeman. "Sorry to startle you, but for a moment there I thought you might be burglars . . ." "So you're convinced the necklace is still here too?" asks Watson. "That's right," nods Growler. "If Timkins is telling the truth, then I think the thief might come back to collect his swag from wherever it's hidden . . ." "Shhh!" hisses Rupert. "He may be here already. We mustn't do anything to let him know we suspect . . ."

RUPERT SPOTS THE THIEF

He sprinkles powder, that he found
In Holmes's lab, upon the ground.

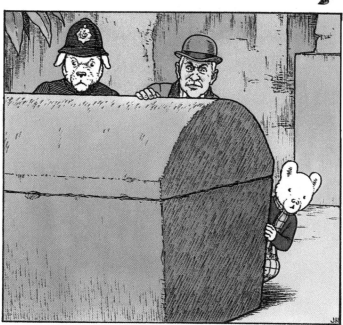

"Take cover now, please, everyone!
Our evening vigil's just begun . . ."

At first it seems that no-one's there,
Then creaking noises fill the air . . .

A mummy case swings open wide.
The thief emerges from inside!

To the others' surprise, Rupert takes a small jar from Dr. Watson's bag and sprinkles some powder in the doorway of the exhibition room. "What's he up to?" whispers Growler. "It's something from Holmes's laboratory," explains Watson. "But I don't know how it's going to help us catch the thief . . ." "Time to take cover," announces Rupert. "It's important the thief doesn't spot us!" "Very well," agrees Watson. "We'll keep watch from behind this stone sarcophagus . . ."

For a long time nothing happens, then Rupert hears a strange creaking sound . . . "Great Scott!" gasps Dr. Watson. "It's coming from one of the mummy cases!" "Don't move!" whispers Rupert. The next moment the front of the mummy case swings open and a wiry-looking man comes running straight towards them. "The thief!" cries Rupert. "I knew he'd be hiding somewhere!" "Well done!" says Sergeant Growler. "Time I took over now. Our friend doesn't look the sort to give up without a struggle . . ."

RUPERT MAKES A SUGGESTION

"Stop!" Growler calls and blocks the way.
The thief stares back in shocked dismay.

He charges forward with a cry
And, pushing Watson, hurries by.

"Gone!" Growler blinks. "I don't know how
We'll find out where he's hiding now!"

"Turn out your lamp and then you'll see
Exactly where the thief must be . . ."

"Stop!" calls Growler, blowing on his whistle as he steps out from behind the sarcophagus. The thief seems dazzled by his lantern and halts for a moment, only to charge forward as Growler and Watson hurry to block the way. "You won't get away with this!" warns Dr. Watson as the man draws level. "Says you!" laughs the thief and pushes him out of the way. "Sergeant flatfoot and his men will never be able to find me in the dark!" he jeers and runs off into the gloom.

By the time Growler picks himself up, the thief has vanished from sight. "I'm afraid he's right!" sighs the policeman. "He could be hiding behind any of these statues . . . it would take us forever to search the whole museum." "We shouldn't have to!" smiles Rupert. "There's a much quicker way of finding the thief than that . . ." "What do you mean?" asks Growler. "He's given us the slip and that's that!" "Perhaps not!" says Rupert. "Turn out your lantern, then tell me what you see . . ."

RUPERT RECOVERS THE NECKLACE

"Footprints!" gasps Growler. "Well I'm blowed!
I'd no idea that powder glowed."

"Well done!" laughs Watson. "Clever you!
It's just what Sherlock Holmes would do!"

The trail leads Growler to the thief
Who shakes his head in disbelief . . .

He hands the necklace back and groans.
"Must be the world's most precious stones!"

"Footprints!" cries Growler. "There's a trail of footprints, glowing in the dark . . ." "Exactly!" says Rupert. "The thief ran through a patch of luminous powder I sprinkled in the doorway. Wherever he goes, he'll leave a set of footprints we can see in the dark!" "Ingenious!" chuckles Dr. Watson. "So that's what you wanted from Holmes's laboratory. It's just the sort of thing he might have done himself . . ." "Come on!" says Growler. "Let's see where our burglar is hiding this time . . ."

As they follow the trail of footprints, Sergeant Growler suddenly starts to smile. "It's a dead end!" he tells Rupert. "Our friend has run out of places to hide!" Sure enough, when Growler lights his lamp, the thief is revealed, skulking in a corner of the room. "It's a fair cop!" he shrugs. "Though I don't know how you found me!" "Hand over the Pharaoh's Treasure!" demands Dr. Watson. The crook produces the gleaming necklace from the folds of his jacket. "Must be worth a fortune!" he sighs.

RUPERT MEETS SHERLOCK HOLMES

Next morning, Sherlock Holmes looks in
And waves the paper, with a grin.

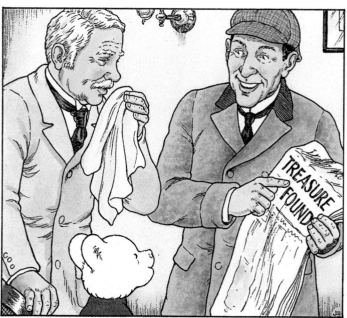

"Good work, Watson!" he calls. "I see
You've solved this Pharaoh mystery!"

"I'm still intrigued our friend was sure
The treasure would be found once more . . ."

"Of course!" smiles Holmes. "You come from when
The treasure's on display again!"

Next morning, Rupert and Watson are still having breakfast when a familiar figure appears in the doorway . . . "Holmes!" cries Dr. Watson. "You're back from your holiday!" "Yes!" laughs the famous detective. "But I see from the papers that you've been managing very well without me . . ." "Ah," smiles Watson. "I'm afraid I can't take any credit for that. It was Rupert here who solved the crime!" "So I gather," says Holmes. "Splendid work, young man. You must tell me all about it, after breakfast."

"You did well to deduce that the thief was hiding inside the museum," says Holmes. "But I'm intrigued you were so certain the necklace would be recovered." "I saw it in the exhibition!" says Rupert. "Indeed?" muses Holmes. "Of course! *After* it was meant to have been stolen!" "What?" gasps Watson. "Elementary!" declares Holmes. "Not only is our young friend an excellent detective, but a time traveller too! Now he's found the Pharaoh's Treasure, he'll want to be getting home . . ."

RUPERT FINDS THE TIME MACHINE

Holmes says he thinks he knows a way
Of getting to the Present Day . . .

"Meet Mr. Wells! His new device
Should travel through time in a trice!"

Wells leads them to his new machine –
It's one Rupert's already seen!

"Just set the year and hold on tight!
We'll find out if my theory's right . . ."

As Sherlock Holmes has guessed his secret, Rupert tells him how he came to travel back in time. "I'd like to return to my own century, but don't know how!" he sighs. "A friend of mine might be able to help you," smiles Holmes. "Young fellow by the name of Wells. He's been tinkering with a time machine for ages . . . Let's go and see if it really works!" Bidding farewell to Watson and Mrs. Hudson, Rupert follows Holmes outside and is soon at the door of Wells's workshop . . .

Inside the workshop Rupert is astonished to see the same machine he found in the Science Museum! "This is it," declares Wells. "The very first vehicle of its kind! At the turn of a dial it can send you back or forward in time, to whichever year you choose..." "Exactly what we need!" cries Holmes. He explains where Rupert has come from and how he wants to return to the Twentieth century. "Nothing simpler!" says Wells. "Just hold on tight!" He presses a button and the time machine begins to hum . . .

RUPERT RETURNS SAFELY

"Goodbye!" calls Holmes, then disappears
As Rupert spins across the years . . .

The journey ends and Rupert comes
Straight back to where he left his chums.

"What happened?" Bingo asks. "I saw
You vanish, then come back, I'm sure!"

He tells his two chums what occurred,
Convinced they won't believe a word!

"It's working!" cries Wells as the hum of the machine growls louder and louder. "Goodbye!" calls Holmes, waving to Rupert, who finds himself spinning through the clouds and stars, back to the present day . . . At last, the mist clears and he recognises his chums, still standing in exactly the same spot as when he left them. "Rupert!" gasps Ottoline. "Thank goodness you're safe. The machine started to make a noise and for a moment we both thought you'd disappeared!"

"Disappeared?" asks Rupert as he climbs down from the time machine to join his puzzled chums. "Was I gone for very long?" "No," blinks Bingo. "But I'm *certain* you vanished for a second or two . . . Tell us what really happened!" "I'm not sure you'd believe me if I did!" laughs Rupert, as Dr. Chimp calls them to come and join the others. "Let's just say that everything's finally ended up exactly where it should be – including me!"

THE END

RUPERT and

The Bears are on a holiday
By the seaside – at Rocky Bay.

It is the height of summer and Rupert and his parents have just arrived at Rocky Bay. "What a beautiful day," smiles Mrs. Bear as they set off for a stroll. "I do hope it stays as fine as this for the rest of the week." As they make their way down to the beach, Rupert suddenly spots somebody he knows. "Cap'n Binnacle!" he cries and waves excitedly to his old friend, who blinks with surprise, then turns round to see who is there . . .

the Star Gazer

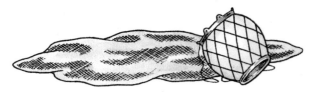

As Rupert walks along the street
He spots someone he's glad to meet . . .

It's Captain Binnacle, who cries,
"Ahoy! I'm weighed down with supplies!"

Cap'n Binnacle is a kindly old sailor who knows Rupert from his previous visits to Rocky Bay. "Ahoy there!" he puffs. "Can't stop, I'm afraid. Got a heavy cargo on board . . ." "You have got rather a lot of shopping," says Rupert. "Perhaps I could help you to carry it home." "Thank you!" says the Cap'n and hands Rupert a bulky parcel. "We'll wait for you on the beach," calls Mr. Bear as Rupert sets off towards the old man's cabin.

"I'll help you!" Rupert says. "Let's share . . ."
"We'll wait down here," says Mr. Bear.

RUPERT IS PROMISED A LESSON

The Captain climbs a winding track
Which leads up to his cliff-top shack.

Inside are lots of things to see
But what can this brass object be?

"A sextant! How we sailors steer
When darkness falls and stars appear . . ."

"I'll show you later. Come back when
It's dark. There should be stars out then!"

To Rupert's delight, Cap'n Binnacle's shack is just as he remembers. Perched high on a rocky outcrop, overlooking the sea, it is crammed full of all sorts of treasures, from cuttlefish to compasses, starfish to shells . . . "Have a look round!" smiles the Cap'n as he unpacks his shopping. "Everything here is to do with the sea." "What's that?" asks Rupert, pointing to a brass object lying on a shelf. "A sextant!" says his friend. "It helps us sailors find our way."

Cap'n Binnacle holds up the sextant for Rupert to see. "It's what we use to steer by the stars!" he explains. "If you're far away from land, they're the only things that show you where you are. You have to take a careful sighting, then check it against your chart." "So sailors never get lost!" marvels Rupert. "They *shouldn't* if the stars are clear," chuckles the Captain. "Come back this evening and I'll show you how it works." "Thanks!" cries Rupert. "I'll ask my parents straightaway . . ."

When Mr. Bear hears what his son
Has planned, he thinks it sounds like fun . . .

The pair set off. "A perfect night!
There's not a single cloud in sight!"

They near the shack, then hear a shout
Of greeting as their friend steps out.

"This sextant's been on every trip
I've ever made aboard a ship!"

Hurrying to the beach, Rupert tells his parents all about the Captain's sextant. "He's offered to show me how it works," he explains. "What fun!" smiles Mr. Bear. "A spot of star gazing sounds just the thing for a summer's evening . . ." As soon as supper is over, Rupert and his father set off along the deserted streets of Rocky Bay. The stars are already twinkling in the sky and all they can hear is the lapping of the waves. "Perfect!" cries Rupert. "Not a cloud in sight . . ."

Clambering up to Cap'n Binnacle's cabin, Rupert and his father soon spot their old friend, waiting for them to arrive. "Ahoy there!" he calls. " 'Tis a fine night for navigation . . ." Telling the pair to wait outside, he disappears into his cabin and comes back clutching the sextant. "Been with me on every voyage!" declares the old man proudly. "More years than I can remember and never let me down! Now then, Rupert, this is the eye-piece. Take a good look . . ."

RUPERT COUNTS THE STARS

*"Look through the eye-piece carefully
Then tell me which stars you can see . . ."*

*"The Pole Star shows where North must lie,
The Plough's the next sign in the sky."*

*"There are more constellations too.
I'll try to point them out for you . . ."*

*"Two twins and seven Sisters. No –
Six stars! But they can't come and go!"*

"Try to find the Pole Star!" says Cap'n Binnacle as Rupert peers through the sextant. "It shows us where North lies . . ." "Straight ahead!" cries Rupert excitedly. "I say!" laughs Mr. Bear, "Isn't that the Plough?" "Where?" blinks Rupert. "Next to the Pole Star," says Cap'n Binnacle. "Folks used to think stars looked like pictures in the sky – so they gave them all names, like Orion's Belt or the Great Bear . . ." "It's a giant game of join-the-dots!" laughs Rupert's father.

As they gaze at the night sky, Mr. Bear and Cap'n Binnacle spot more constellations. "There's Gemini!" the Captain declares. "Castor and Pollux!" chuckles Mr. Bear. "My father showed me those when I was no bigger than Rupert . . ." "The cluster over there is called the Seven Sisters," explain Cap'n Binnacle. "But there are only six!" says Rupert. "Six?" gasps the Captain. "There can't be!" Peering up, he starts to count them one by one. "Bless me, Rupert. You're right!"

RUPERT HEARS ONE IS MISSING

"The strongest telescope I've got!
Let's try again and count the lot . . ."

"Still six stars!" Rupert's father tries.
"I only see six too!" he cries.

They leave the Captain, still perplexed.
"Six stars!" he groans. "Whatever next?"

Next day, Rupert's keen to explore
Some rock pools he's seen by the shore.

Hurrying into his cabin, Cap'n Binnacle fetches a powerful telescope and peers at the twinkling stars. "Six Sisters!" he murmurs. "My old eyes must be playing tricks . . ." Mr. Bear has a look through the telescope, but he can only see six stars too. "How odd!" he shrugs. "There were definitely seven last time I looked." "What's the world coming to?" sighs Cap'n Binnacle. "If sailors can't rely on stars any longer, how will they be able to find their way?"

Cap'n Binnacle is still staring at the stars in disbelief as Rupert and his father bid him farewell and set off back to their hotel. "It's all very strange," says Mr. Bear. "Stars don't just disappear . . . but one of the Seven Sisters really seems to have vanished." Despite his late night, Rupert is up bright and early the next morning to go and play on the beach. "I wonder if the tide's out?" he thinks. "Rocky Bay has some marvellous pools for exploring . . ."

RUPERT FINDS A LANTERN

He kneels down, trying hard to reach,
Then spots an object on the beach.

"A ball or glass float of some kind!
It's been washed up then left behind . . ."

"It's not a float! A lantern? Why!
It's parachuted from the sky!"

He takes the lantern back to show
His parents. "Maybe they might know?"

To Rupert's delight, the tide is on its way out and he soon has the whole beach to explore. Delving into a rockpool with his net, he suddenly spots something peculiar lying on the sand. "It's a glass ball," he thinks as he goes to take a closer look. "But what's this tied to it?" To Rupert's surprise, the folds of silky material look just like a little parachute. "Goodness!" he blinks. "I wonder where it's from? It must have been washed up on the beach during the night . . ."

Rupert picks up the mysterious object, only to find that it isn't a ball at all . . . "It's more like a glass lantern!" he gasps. Peering inside, he can see the charred wick of what looks like a burnt-down candle. "I wonder what it's for?" he thinks. "Why is there a parachute tied to the rim, and how did it come to be in Rocky Bar?" Rupert decides to take the lantern back to show his parents. "If they don't know, then perhaps Cap'n Binnacle might," he thinks.

"Look!" Rupert cries. "This lamp I found
Was lying, stranded on the ground . . ."

"I wonder?" murmurs Mr. Bear.
"An aircraft might have dropped a flare . . ."

"Show Binnacle when lunch is done.
He might have found another one!"

Intrigued to think there might be more,
Rupert sets off to search the shore.

When Rupert arrives at the hotel, his parents have just finished packing a picnic. "Did you have a nice walk?" asks Mrs. Bear. "Yes," says Rupert, "and look what I found!" "What is it?" asks his mother. "I don't know," says Rupert. "Some sort of lantern, I think . . ." "Perhaps it fell from an aeroplane?" suggests Mr. Bear. "It could be a flare to show you where you're flying at night. That would explain the parachute – although I've never seen one before . . ."

Now that the picnic is ready, the Bears set off towards the beach. "We'll take the lantern with us," says Mr. Bear. "You can show it to Cap'n Binnacle later, in case he knows what it's for . . ." Choosing a spot near the water's edge, they settle down, while Rupert goes off for another walk. "I just want to take a closer look where the lantern landed," he explains. "There might be some clues to where it came from . . ." "Take care!" calls Mrs. Bear. "And don't be gone too long . . ."

33

RUPERT MEETS A STRANGER

Exactly where the lantern fell,
He finds a little girl as well . . .

"Hello!" she smiles. "Will you agree
To join in searching here, with me?"

"Of course!" smiles Rupert. Then he blinks.
"She's got a silver crown!" he thinks.

"I know the thing you're looking for –
The lamp I found here by the shore!"

As Rupert approaches the place where he found the lantern, he sees a little girl coming along the beach towards him. She seems to be looking for something and peers so intently at the sand that she doesn't notice him until they are nearly level. "Hello!" says Rupert, marvelling at her shimmering dress and silver crown. "Hello!" smiles the girl. "You're the first person I've met from Rocky Bay! Perhaps you can help me? I've come to recover something very important."

"Of course I'll help you," says Rupert. "Although I'm not actually *from* Rocky Bay, I'm only staying here on holiday . . ." "Holiday?" blinks the girl. "What's that?" Rupert begins to explain, when he suddenly realises what she must be searching for. "The lantern!" he gasps. "That's what you've lost, isn't it? It was lying on the beach when I came here this morning . . ." "Yes!" cries the girl excitedly. "Can you tell me where to find it? It's important I get it back before nightfall . . ."

RUPERT RETURNS THE LAMP

"I'll fetch it for you, never fear!
I won't be gone long. Just wait here!"

He runs to get the lamp and then
Sets off along the beach again . . .

"Thank goodness!" cries the girl. "And I'm
Not too late to get back in time!"

"Back where?" blinks Rupert. "Won't you tell?"
"No time!" the girl smiles. "Come as well!"

The girl seems so keen to recover the lamp that Rupert decides to run and fetch it straightaway. "Wait here!" he calls. "I'll be back as soon as I can . . ." Hurrying to where his parents are having the picnic, he quickly tells them that he has found the lantern's owner, searching for it on the beach. "Who is it?" asks Mrs. Bear. "No time to explain!" calls Rupert as he runs off with the lamp. "She seems in a dreadful hurry. I promised to bring it back as quickly as I could . . ."

When Rupert returns with the lamp, the little girl is overjoyed. "Wonderful!" she cries. "Thank goodness it isn't damaged. I'd better set off immediately . . ." "Wait!" calls Rupert. "Where are you going, and why is the lamp so important? At least tell me that before you go!" "Sorry," says the girl. "There's no time! I can't risk being late." Seeing Rupert's disappointment, she stops, then gives a broad smile. "Why don't you come with me? Then you'll understand everything . . ."

RUPERT SEES A FLYING HORSE

"My name is Stella. Follow me.
There's someone else here you should see!"

"Meet Pegasus – my trusty steed!
He takes me everywhere I need . . ."

"He flew at full speed all the way
Until we came to Rocky Bay."

"I'm sure he won't mind taking you.
My chariot's just right for two . . ."

Following the girl along the beach, Rupert tells her his name and how he lives in a village called Nutwood. "My name's Stella," she replies. "You'll see where I live when we reach our journey's end . . ." Before she can say more, the pair round the headland and Rupert sees a beautiful winged horse, with a gleaming silver chariot. "Pegasus!" calls Stella. "I've found what we came for! Come and say hello," she tells Rupert. "Pegasus has never met a bear before . . ."

Stella introduces Rupert to the winged horse. "He's mine!" she says proudly. "Pegasus and I go everywhere together." "Can he really fly?" asks Rupert. "Of course," she smiles. "That's how we came to Rocky Bay. It was a long way, but Pegasus didn't even stop for a rest." The silver chariot is just big enough for the two of them to stand side by side. "Don't forget to hold on!" warns Stella as she takes up Pegasus' reins. "He's a gentle creature really, but faster than the wind . . ."

RUPERT HAS A RIDE

The white horse flaps its wings. The pair
Take off and soar into the air!

"Amazing!" Rupert cries aloud,
As up they gallop, through the cloud.

Ahead he spots a building where
His new friend lives. "We're nearly there . . ."

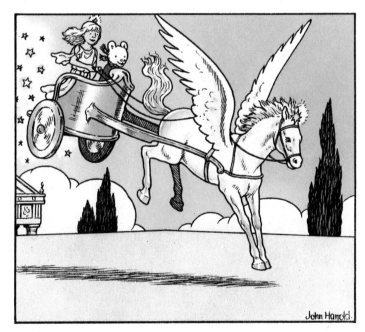

"I hope that you enjoyed the ride!
We'll meet my sisters now, inside . . ."

As soon as Rupert is safely aboard, the white horse begins to gallop along the beach. Beating the air with its mighty wings, it suddenly leaps up and soars into the sky. "Gosh!" marvels Rupert. "I can see the whole of Rocky Bay. It looks like a model village!" In no time at all they have left the coast behind them and speed out across the sea. Up and up flies Pegasus until they burst through the clouds into dazzling sunshine. "Bravo!" laughs Stella. "We're on our way . . ."

With Pegasus pulling the chariot as fast as he can, Rupert and Stella speed through the sky in a shimmering trail of stars. Peering eagerly ahead, Rupert spots a distant building, perched on top of fleecy clouds. "That's where I live!" smiles Stella. "We can see Rocky Bay through a huge telescope at the top of my father's tower." Pegasus swoops down and lands in an open courtyard. "Come and meet my sisters!" says Stella. "We don't get many visitors from down below . . ."

RUPERT FOLLOWS STELLA

*"I'll introduce you later when
My father knows we're back again."*

*"Hello! Papa's expecting you.
He saw you fly back into view . . ."*

*"This way!" says Stella. "He must be
At work in the Observatory."*

*"My father watches stars all night.
Then goes to sleep when it gets light . . ."*

Leaving Pegasus in the courtyard, Stella leads the way to the main tower. As he climbs the steps, Rupert spots two girls, polishing a large telescope. "My sisters!" smiles Stella. "I'll introduce you later, but first I've got to let my father know I'm back." Inside the tower there are all sorts of astronomical instruments and charts. Another of Stella's sisters is busy dusting a model of the planets. "Father's expecting you," she says. "He saw Pegasus returning . . ."

"My father's observatory is at the top of the tower," explains Stella as they climb a steep flight of steps. "He has a clear view of the stars from there and watches them all night." "When does he sleep?" asks Rupert. "During the day," says Stella. "We only ever see him in the afternoon." When they reach the top of the tower, she stops and knocks at a closed door. "If he spotted Pegasus, he'll be awake," she whispers. "He will be pleased when he sees what I've brought . . ."

RUPERT MEETS THE STAR GAZER

"Come in!" a voice calls. "Hello, dear!
I've still to check these Star Charts here . . ."

"What's this you've brought me back? I say!
The one we lost near Rocky Bay!"

"My friend's the one who found it there.
He comes from Nutwood – Rupert Bear!"

"A welcome guest! I'll tell you all
About the lamps and why they fall . . ."

"Come in!" calls a kindly voice. Rupert follows Stella into the room where her father is studying charts of the sky. "So many stars," he murmurs. "Some of them aren't even marked yet, you know . . ." "Papa!" cries Stella. "Look what I've found. It's the lantern that fell into the sea near Rocky Bay . . ." "Gracious!" he blinks. "You have done well! I'd almost given it up for lost. How ever did you manage to find it so quickly? And who's this you've brought with you?"

"This is my new friend, Rupert," says Stella. "He found the lantern, lying on the beach at Rocky Bay . . ." "Pleased to meet you," says Stella's father. "I wonder if you realise exactly what it is you've helped to recover?" "No!" says Rupert. "I can see it's some sort of lamp, but I can't imagine what the little parachute is for . . ." "All in good time," smiles Stella's father. "First you need to know who we are and why we spend so many evenings searching the heavens for stars . . ."

RUPERT LEARNS ABOUT STARS

*"Each lantern is an evening star
That folk see shining from afar . . ."*

*"My job's to watch them through the night
And make sure that they stay alight!"*

*"If one should fall, we find it, then
Replace it in the sky again."*

*"Come on!" says Stella. "We'll be late
For Pegasus. He said he'd wait . . ."*

"They call me the Star Gazer," says Stella's father. "It's my job to make sure every star keeps burning in the sky . . ." "You mean the stars are all lanterns?" gasps Rupert. "Exactly!" he smiles. "The one you found had burnt down too low. As soon as their flame goes out, they fall to earth . . ." Unscrewing the base of the lamp, he shows Rupert the remains of a tiny candle. "It's time for a new one as soon as a star starts to flicker," he explains. "That's what I try to spot . . ."

"To think that *I* found a star!" marvels Rupert. "Cap'n Binnacle will never believe me!" "You can help me put it back if you like," says Stella. "We ought to be setting off soon, before it gets dark . . ." "Farewell, little bear!" smiles the Star Gazer. "Your help will not be forgotten." "Goodbye," says Rupert. "And thank you for explaining about the lamp. I'll think of you each time I see a star . . ." "Come on!" calls Stella. "We mustn't keep Pegasus waiting any longer."

RUPERT MAKES ANOTHER JOURNEY

The chariot's all ready for
The pair to ride away once more.

"Towards the stars now!" Stella cries,
As Pegasus takes off and flies.

The sky grows dark and stars appear.
"Look!" Stella calls. "We're getting near!"

"So many lanterns!" Rupert blinks.
"I'm sure I'd lose my way!" he thinks.

Down in the courtyard, two of Stella's sisters are waiting by the silver chariot. One holds a slender pole, while the other has a box full of candles. "Rupert's coming with me," says Stella. "As the person who found the missing star, it's only right that he should help to put it back." Climbing aboard, she urges Pegasus on his way. The white horse bounds forward and soars into the sky on outstretched wings. "Up to the stars!" calls Stella. "As quickly as you can . . ."

As Pegasus speeds on, Rupert and Stella leave the Observatory behind and climb above the last wisps of cloud. The sky grows dark as night approaches and ahead of them Rupert spots some glimmering points of light. "More lanterns!" he cries. "That's right!" laughs Stella. "They're the first stars . . ." Soon the sky is full of bright spheres, all hanging from little parachutes. "How do you know where to go?" asks Rupert. "From the Star Chart!" says Stella. "Up here we use it like a map . . ."

Rupert and the Star Gazer

Rupert and the Star Gazer

RUPERT'S FRIEND FINDS THE WAY

"A Star Chart shows exactly where
The lantern's needed . . . over there!"

"The seventh Sister! So that's why
We only saw six in the sky!"

"Stop!" Stella calls. "I see a space.
We'll try to set the star in place . . ."

"These candles last a century.
There's one in every star you see!"

Unrolling the chart, Stella shows Rupert how all the constellations are clearly marked, together with a winding path which twists and turns between them. "There are the Seven Sisters," she declares. "Keep going, Pegasus! We should be able to see them soon . . ." Sure enough, as Rupert peers at the twinkling stars, he sees a cluster of six lanterns shimmering in the distance. "There will soon be seven again," smiles Rupert. "I wonder if Cap'n Binnacle is looking up through his telescope?"

When they reach the constellation, Rupert can see a large gap where the seventh star should be. "We won't take long," Stella tells Pegasus and hands the missing lantern to Rupert. "All it needs is a new candle," she smiles. "Do you replace them very often?" asks Rupert. "Oh, no!" laughs Stella. "This one should last for a hundred years. If they burnt any quicker my father's job would be impossible. Some stars last even longer, it all depends on how brightly they shine . . ."

42

RUPERT HELPS TO LAUNCH A STAR

Then Stella lights the candle so
The missing star begins to glow . . .

The parachute fills with hot air
And floats away, above the pair.

As Rupert watches, Stella steers
The star in place. "That's it!" she cheers.

Then, as they leave, there's one last chance
To give the stars a backward glance . . .

Lighting the lantern with a small wax taper, Stella tells Rupert to hold the parachute open. "We've got to let it fill up with hot air," she explains. The lamp grows brighter and brighter, until Rupert finds its glow quite dazzling. "The parachute's ready now!" calls Stella. "Let's see if it still works . . ." The pair let go of the lamp which, to Rupert's delight, starts to drift slowly higher and higher into the sky. "Bravo!" laughs Stella. "It's almost back where it should be."

Now that the missing star is back in the sky, all that remains is for Rupert and Stella to steer it into place. "That's what the pole is for," she says. "Stars often drift off course . . ." When everything is ready, Stella tells Pegasus to fly on to Rocky Bay. "Time you were getting home," she says. "Everyone must be wondering where you are!" Rupert agrees, but can't resist a backward glance as the chariot speeds away. "*Seven* sisters!" he smiles and counts them, one by one . . .

RUPERT FLIES HOME

Back through the night the pair return,
Past stars that twinkle as they burn.

Then Pegasus swoops gently down
Towards a tiny coastal town . . .

"Thanks, once again, for all you've done!"
"Thank you!" smiles Rupert. "I've had fun!"

He waits, then turns to wave goodbye
As Stella shoots across the sky.

As Rupert and Stella travel back to Rocky Bay the sky is full of stars, which gleam and twinkle on every side. "The darker it gets, the more you can see!" gasps Rupert. "No need for a chart now," laughs Stella. "Pegasus can find the way back all by himself . . ." In no time at all the flying horse swoops down with an excited whinny. "It's Rocky Bay!" cries Rupert. "There's the sea – and I can see the lights of all the houses." "We'll land on the beach," says Stella, "where you found the lamp . . ."

Leaving the chariot at the far end of the beach, Stella climbs out to bid Rupert farewell. "Thank you for helping us," she says. "Thank you," smiles Rupert. "I'm glad I came with you to put the star back. All those glowing lanterns were a wonderful sight!" As he sets off along the shore, Rupert glances back and sees Pegasus soaring into the night sky. "Goodbye," he calls, waving after the chariot, then hurries on his way to Rocky Bay to let everyone know that he is safe and sound.

Rupert and the Star Gazer

RUPERT'S PARENTS SEE ALL'S WELL

Then Rupert hurries back to see
His parents searching anxiously . . .

"I'm sorry, but I didn't know
My new friend had so far to go!"

"The stars look clear!" says Mr. Bear.
"Now there are seven Sisters there!"

The Captain smiles. "I see them too!
That's good. Six stars would never do!"

As Rupert nears the main beach, he spots his parents and Cap'n Binnacle "Hello!" he calls. "Sorry I took so long . . ." "Wherever have you been?" asks Mrs. Bear. "Returning the lamp," explains Rupert. "Must have been a long way," says Cap'n Binnacle. "We searched the beach but couldn't find you anywhere . . ." "It *was* a long way," says Rupert. "But at least the lantern's safely back." "So are you!" smiled Mr. Bear. "That's the main thing, though next time don't go so far . . ."

On the way back to their hotel, Mr. Bear stops for a last look out to sea. "I say!" he cries. "The stars are clear tonight! Look at the Seven Sisters…" Everyone stares up at the twinkling points of light. "Bless me!" gasps Cap'n Binnacle. "I can see all seven this time. My old eyes must have been playing tricks on me before. Fancy thinking that stars could come and go . . ." Rupert smiles gently to himself, but doesn't say a word . . .

THE END

RUPERT and

*The farmer's asked the pals if they
Can help him gather in the hay.*

It is nearly the end of summer. Rupert and his pals are helping Farmer Brown to gather the last of this year's hay. They have been working busily since early morning, loading the freshly–mown hay on to a large wagon. "Well done, lads!" calls the farmer. "We've got it all in before the rain!" Farmer Brown is so pleased he asks Rupert, Bill and Algy back to the farmhouse for tea. "Mrs. Brown promised to bake a special cake!" he smiles.

46

Odmedod's Adventure

*"Well done!" he smiles. "Now I think we
Deserve a special farmhouse tea . . ."*

*"Climb up!" he calls. "Sit side by side.
I'll give you all a wagon ride!"*

Rupert and his chums perch high on top of the
hay wagon as Farmer Brown sets off across the
fields. He leads his horse along winding lanes until
they see the farmhouse, on the very outskirts of
Nutwood. To their surprise, the pals find Mrs.
Brown has set up a table in the courtyard outside.
"I thought it would be nice to have a picnic," she
smiles. "You must be hungry after working so
hard. Come and have some lemonade . . ."

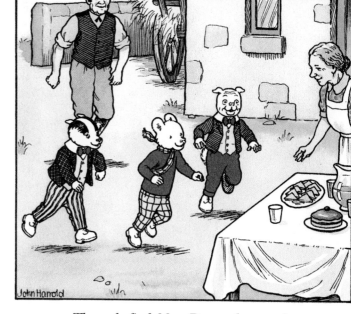

*The pals find Mrs. Brown has made
Some sandwiches and lemonade.*

47

RUPERT SPOTS ODMEDOD

"My wife has baked a sponge cake too!"
The farmer smiles. "It's all for you . . ."

Then Rupert spots his scarecrow chum.
"It's Odmedod! But why's he glum?"

"Hello! What's wrong? You look so sad!
I hope it isn't something bad!"

"It's Autumn!" Odmedod replies.
"The birds have all flown off!" he sighs.

"Eat as much as you like," smiles Farmer Brown as he cuts the cake. "You deserve a treat for all you've done today. My cows will be glad of the hay we've gathered when it comes to the depths of winter . . ." As the pals enjoy their lemonade, Rupert suddenly catches sight of somebody he knows. "Odmedod!" he gasps, staring at the farmer's scarecrow. But why is his chum propped up in a corner of the yard rather than standing out in the fields? And why is he looking so glum?

Slipping away from the others, Rupert asks Odmedod what has happened. "Why are you here?" he whispers. "What's the matter?" "Hello!" says the scarecrow gloomily. "It's the end of summer, that's what! Now everything has been harvested, there's nothing left for me to guard. Farmer Brown brings me in for winter. While all the birds fly off to somewhere nice and warm, I spend winter in a dreary old barn!" sighs Odmedod. "I'd like to go on holiday too. It's not fair!"

RUPERT HAS AN IDEA

"Poor Odmedod! Left all alone . . .
I wonder where the birds have flown?"

"The birds fly South, across the sea."
Says Mrs. Bear. "That's where they'll be!"

First thing, next morning, Rupert goes
To find out what the Wise Owl knows . . .

"Your scarecrow friend could go South too!
Ask Sailor Sam if he'll help you."

"Poor Odmedod!" thinks Rupert as he goes to join his pals. "I never thought about how he spends the winter. He must be lonely without the birds for company. Farmer Brown doesn't know they're his best friends . . ." Later that evening, as he is getting ready for bed, Rupert asks his mother where Nutwood's birds all go in the winter. "South!" she explains. "They fly across the sea to where it's warm and sunny. Some go all the way to Africa, hundreds and hundreds of miles . . ."

Next morning, Rupert decides to help Odmedod join the migrating birds. He sets off across the common in search of the Wise Old Owl. "Hello!" blinks the owl. "You're up very early!" "I've come to ask your advice," says Rupert and tells him what Odmedod wants . . . "No reason why a scarecrow shouldn't go South," nods the owl. "The only problem is how to get there! He can't fly, so you'd better find someone who owns a boat. How about Sailor Sam? Why don't you ask him?"

Rupert climbs up a winding track,
Across the common, to Sam's shack.

The sailor's ready to begin
A voyage. "Why don't you both join in?"

"You ask your Mum if it's all right,
Then we'll leave for the coast tonight!"

"Of course!" smiles Mrs. Bear. "Sam's bound
To bring you back home, safe and sound."

Rupert does as the Wise Owl suggests and sets off towards Sailor Sam's cabin on the edge of Nutwood. When he gets there, he finds his friend is already busy packing for a voyage . . . "I'm just off in search of warmer climes," he smiles. "Nutwood winters are far too chilly for the likes of me!" When he hears how Odmedod wants to go South, he soon agrees to take the scarecrow with him. "Why don't you come too?" he asks Rupert. "You can ask your mother while I finish packing . . ."

"We'll set off for the coast this evening," Sam calls as Rupert hurries away. "Bring Odmedod with you as soon as it starts to get dark . . ." Mrs. Bear knows that Sam always takes good care of Rupert And agrees to let him go on a special voyage. "We'll be taking another friend with us," adds Rupert, but doesn't mention Odmedod's name, as his mother, like most people in Nutwood, has never seen the scarecrow move and doesn't even know that he can talk.

Rupert runs to the farm, but where
Is Odmedod? There's no-one there . . .

"Perhaps he's in the barn? I'll call
And see if he's in here at all . . ."

The scarecrow answers. "Over here!
My work's all finished for the year!"

"Good!" Rupert smiles. "Then you'll be free
To come with Sailor Sam and me!"

While Mrs. Bear looks out some spare clothes, Rupert goes to tell Odmedod how Sam has agreed to take them on a special voyage. He reaches Farmer Brown's house, only to find the farmyard deserted and no sign of the scarecrow anywhere. "I wonder where he's got to?" thinks Rupert. "I didn't see him in the fields . . ." Pushing open the door of the barn, he gently calls out Odmedod's name. "Are you there?" he hisses. "It's Rupert. I've come to tell you some good news . . ."

Rupert hears an answering call from inside the gloomy barn. "Over here!" cries Odmedod, throwing off a tarpaulin. "I've been put away for the winter!" "Good!" smiles Rupert. "If your work is done for the year, then you can come with me on an ocean voyage . . ." "Really?" beams the scarecrow. "That would be wonderful!" "Sailor Sam's agreed to take us both," explains Rupert. "He's leaving as soon as it's dark but first we'll have to make sure nobody sees you've gone . . ."

Rupert and Odmedod's Adventure

RUPERT'S PAL ARRIVES

"You won't be missed, but just in case,
We'll leave this old broom in your place!"

"We'll meet up later by Sam's shack!"
Calls Rupert as he hurries back.

"Ahoy there!" Sam calls. "I'm all set,
But no sight of your chum, just yet!"

Then Odmedod arrives. He's been
The long way round "So I'm not seen!"

Although Farmer Brown doesn't need Odmedod during winter, Rupert knows he'd still be worried if he thought the scarecrow was missing. "I know!" he cries. "We'll put this broom under the tarpaulin, then no one will ever know you've gone. We don't need to be at Sam's cabin until nightfall, so you can slip away at twilight without being seen..." "Thanks, Rupert!" says Odmedod. "I can't believe I'm really going!" "See you later," calls Rupert and hurries back to finish packing...

By the time the sky grows dark, Rupert has bid his parents farewell and hurries along to Sam's cabin. "Ahoy, there!" calls the sailor. "No sign of your chum yet! Come in and have some tea while we're waiting for him to arrive..." Before long, Rupert hears an anxious knock at Sam's front door. "Hello!" smiles Odmedod. "I hope I'm not late, but I had to come across the fields. People aren't used to seeing me move about, you know!" "Neither am I!" laughs Sam.

52

RUPERT TRAVELS TO THE COAST

The scarecrow thanks Sam gratefully.
"I never dreamt I'd go to sea!"

Sam starts his motorbike. "Hurray!"
Cries Rupert. "Now we're on our way!"

They reach the coast as it gets light.
"Look!" Odmedod calls. "What a sight!"

Sam's boat is tied up, down below.
"I keep her here, all set to go!"

"Thank you for agreeing to take me," says Odmedod as he joins Sam and Rupert. "I've always wanted to see where Nutwood's birds go in the winter!" "Glad you can join us," smiles Sam. "I hope you enjoy the voyage. Let's set off straight away!" Sam's motorbike has a large sidecar which Rupert and Odmedod can share. As soon as they are safely aboard, he starts the engine and speeds off along the empty road. "This is the life!" laughs Sam. "Up and away, while everyone else is sleeping . . ."

As Sam drives through the darkness, Rupert begins to feel drowsy. His head nods, and soon he has fallen asleep. "Wake up!" calls Odmedod as they reach the coast. "The sun's just rising and I can see the sea!" The two chums soon spot Sam's little boat, moored in a rocky harbour down below. "She's called the Venture," he tells them. "Wait a moment and I'll take you both aboard." Rupert and Odmedod gaze out to sea excitedly. "It's even better than I imagined," grins the scarecrow.

RUPERT AND ODMEDOD SET SAIL

"She's called the Venture! Climb aboard,
I'll show you where your things are stored . . ."

They soon set sail - the trip's begun.
"Hurrah!" cries Odmedod. "What fun!"

"We're sailing South!" calls Sam. "I'll start
To plot our journey on my chart."

"A flock of birds!" the scarecrow cries.
"I bet they can't believe their eyes!"

Following Sam down a flight of steps, Rupert and Odmedod clamber aboard the Venture. "Plenty of room for everyone," laughs the sailor. "I'll put your things in the cabin, then we'll unfurl the sails . . ." In no time at all Sam is ready to cast off. "There's a good breeze today," he smiles. "If it stays like this, we're in for an easy voyage." "Hurrah!" cries Odmedod. "I like sailing. It's much better than spending all day in a field . . ." "Well spoken, shipmate!" cries Sam.

Cutting through the water, the Venture soon leaves the coast far behind her and heads out across the open sea. "We're sailing due South!" calls Sam as he plots their course on his chart. "Migrating with the birds!" laughs Rupert. Sure enough, they soon spot a flock of birds, directly overhead. "Ahoy there!" calls Odmedod. "Look at me!" "They're too far away to hear," laughs Sam, but Odmedod is sure his friends have seen him and waves up at them delightedly . . .

RUPERT IS WOKEN BY A STORM

They sail all day, till darkness comes.
"We're halfway there," Sam tells the chums.

"Sleep well, and when you wake again,
I should have sighted land by then!"

When Rupert wakes, he gets a fright.
"It's still the middle of the night!"

A sudden storm has struck the boat –
Sam isn't sure she'll stay afloat!

Rupert and Odmedod are amazed at how big the ocean seems. All day long Sam's little boat speeds on its way, but they never catch a glimpse of land. "Don't worry," laughs Sam. "I can tell where we are from my charts. As long as we keep heading south, we're bound to reach the Tropics!" The sky grows dark as the sun sets, and Sam shows Rupert to his cabin. "Try to get some sleep," he says. "Odmedod can help me keep watch. By the time you wake up we should be nearly there . . ."

Snug in the little cabin, Rupert soon drifts off to sleep. But during the night he is woken by the howling sound of the wind. Peering through the porthole, he can see huge waves braking, and feels the ship being tossed and buffeted by a storm. "Foul weather!" cries Sam as Rupert pulls on his clothes and hurries out to join him. "The Venture's been blown off course and it's all I can do to keep her upright. If things don't calm down soon, I don't know what we'll do . . ."

RUPERT IS WASHED OVERBOARD

*"We'd better put these on, I think.
They'll save us if the ship should sink!"*

*A huge wave strikes. To their dismay
The friends are caught – and washed away!*

*"The Venture!" Sam cries. "Still afloat!
Try clinging to the capsized boat!"*

*"Well done!" he splutters. "Safe at last!
We'll wait here, till the storm has passed."*

As the sea rages angrily, a gust of wind snatches the sail from Sam's grasp. "It's no use!" he cries. "We'll just have to hope for the best!" Disappearing inside, he comes back carrying lifejackets. "You'd better put one on!" he tells Rupert. "It will keep you afloat if the worst comes to the worst!" The next moment a huge wave crashes over the side and sends the three friends reeling. "Look out!" calls Sam, but it's too late. The ship capsizes, hurling them into the sea . . .

Spluttering to the surface, Rupert sees the hull of the Venture floating upsidedown. "Swim towards her!" calls Sam. "We can hold on, like a raft . . ." With his lifejacket keeping him upright, Rupert struggles through the waves until he finally manages to clamber aboard. Sam soon joins him, then reaches out to haul Odmedod to safety. "I can't swim very well!" wails the scarecrow. "Don't worry!" calls Sam. "You'll be fine up here with Rupert. We'll wait for the storm to pass . . ."

RUPERT SPOTS AN ISLAND

*The sea grows calm again, but how
Can Sam tell where they're drifting now?*

*"Look! There's an island I can see!"
Calls Rupert, pointing eagerly.*

*The boat drifts near, then stops once more.
"We'll have to try to swim ashore!"*

*Exhausted, but relieved, they reach
Dry land and flop down on the beach.*

Sure enough, the storm eventually passes over and the sea grows calm once more. The upturned boat makes an excellent raft, but Sam has no idea how far they've been blown off course. "I suppose we're still heading south," he declares, though there is no sign of land. Suddenly, Rupert spots a dark shape on the horizon. "An island!" he gasps. "Look, Sam! We're drifting towards it!" "You're right," cries the sailor. "That's a stroke of luck. If only we can get ashore . . ."

At first the upturned boat drifts slowly towards the island. "We're nearly there!" cheers Rupert, but the chums soon realise that they've stopped moving. "We must have run aground!" says Sam. "I'm afraid we'll have to swim . . ." Plunging into the water, he strikes out for the shore, with Rupert and Odmedod following close behind. When they reach the little island, all three sink down on to the warm sand to recover. "Thank goodness!" gasps Odmedod. "We're back on dry land!"

RUPERT HEARS A PLANE

"Things could be worse!" says Sam. "Let's try
To find some fruit trees, now we're dry."

"We'll need to find fresh water too,
But first, there's something else to do . . ."

"We'll build a shelter from the rain."
Says Sam, but then they hear a plane!

"Stop!" Sam calls, waving frantically.
The plane flies on – too high to see!

After the pals have rested, they decide to set off and explore the island. "At least there are plenty of trees," smiles Sam. "From the look of them, we'll have lots of fruit . . ." Leading the way through thick vegetation, he tells Rupert and Odmedod to stay close together until they are sure the island is safe. "Keep looking for a stream!" he adds. "If we find some fresh water we'll have everything we need. I'll build a shelter we can use until somebody spots us . . ."

The chums have just begun to gather leaves for a shelter when Odmedod hears a low, droning sound. At first he thinks it must be an insect, then he looks up and spots an aeroplane. "Look!" he calls and points it out to the others. Sam scrambles hurriedly to the top of a high rock and waves frantically with his shirt. "Too far away!" he sighs as the plane flies off. "What we really need is a fire to signal with smoke. Planes and ships would be bound to notice that . . ."

RUPERT EXPLORES THE ISLAND

"Don't fret," says Sam. "They'll come again.
We'll have a beacon ready then!"

"The shelter's built. We've done our best!"
Says Sam. "Now try to get some rest."

Next morning, they're refreshed once more.
"I'll make a beacon! You explore . . ."

The pair run off, then stop. "How odd!
Somebody called out Odmedod!"

"Never mind!" says Sam. "There's bound to be another plane, sooner or later. We'll build a shelter first, then make a beacon so we're ready when it comes . . ." Following Sam's instructions, Rupert and Odmedod gather armfuls of leaves to cover a framework of branches. By the time the shelter is finished, the three companions are completely exhausted. "At least we'll stay dry if it rains," says Sam. "Let's get some sleep and explore the rest of the island tomorrow . . ."

Next morning, Rupert wakes up to find the sun already shining. "It's a lovely day!" says Sam. "I'll start work on the beacon, while you two gather some fruit." Rupert and Odmedod begin to search for ripe bananas. Pushing through the tangle of leaves, they find themselves in a forest of tall trees. "I think we should turn back soon," says Rupert, then stops as he hears somebody call Odmedod's name. "Who's that?" gasps the scarecrow. "It didn't sound like Sam . . ."

59

RUPERT MEETS SOME BIRDS

*"A swallow! But I recognise
This Nutwood bird!" the scarecrow cries.*

*The swallow hears how his friend came
To be shipwrecked. "It's such a shame!"*

*Then two white cockatoos appear.
"What's all this talk of wrecks we hear?"*

*"A boat's been washed up here!" they say.
"It's lying in a sheltered bay . . ."*

"Odmedod!" calls a shrill voice. "I'm up here, in the treetops. Look!" To the pals' surprise, the call comes from a swallow, perched high above their heads. "You're from Nutwood!" blinks the scarecrow. "That's right!" chirps the bird. "I'm migrating, but what are *you* doing here?" "We've been shipwrecked!" explains Odmedod and tells how Sailor Sam's boat was swamped by a huge wave. "It was going so well till then," he sighs. "Sam did everything he could, but the sea was too rough!"

As Rupert and Odmedod explain how they were forced to abandon ship and swim to the little island, a pair of white cockatoos fly down to hear their story. "We've just found a boat!" they squawk excitedly. "It's drifted into a bay on the far side of the island." "You mean the Venture isn't wrecked?" asks Rupert. "No!" laugh the birds. "Follow us and we'll take you to see. There's normally nobody here, except for birds, so we've been wondering who it belongs to . . ."

RUPERT FINDS SAM'S BOAT

*The cockatoos fly back to where
They saw the boat. "We'll lead you there!"*

*"The Venture!" Rupert cries. "Let's tell
Sam. He can come and look as well!"*

*"We've made a great discovery!"
calls Rupert. "This way! Follow me . . ."*

*"Bless me!" gasps Sam. "The Venture's found!
It looks as though she's run aground . . ."*

Following the cockatoos as they fly on ahead, Rupert and Odmedod hurry across the island. Jumping over a stream, they reach a rocky valley that leads towards the shore. "It *is* the Venture!" cries Rupert. "Look Odmedod! She's lying on her side. The tide must have carried her here after we swam ashore." "Do you think Sam can save her?" asks Odmedod. "Perhaps," says Rupert. "She doesn't look too badly damaged. Let's go and tell him the news. He'll want to come and see her straightaway..."

By the time Rupert reaches Sam, he is just adding the last leaves to the beacon. "Did you find any fruit for breakfast?" he asks. "No," laughs Rupert. "We've discovered something even better! Come and see..." Although he can't imagine what the pals are up to, Sam follows them across the island until they reach the far shore. "Bless me!" he cries as he spots the Venture. "I never thought I'd see my old ship again! Well done, lads! This is wonderful!"

RUPERT SEES THE VENTURE RIGHTED

Sam wades out to inspect the boat.
How damaged is she? Will she float?

"Astonishing!" they hear him call.
"The Venture's not wrecked, after all!"

"I'll bail her out, then wait a while –
Enjoy a last look round the isle!"

The cockatoos fly off once more.
They've got another treat in store . . .

As Rupert and Odmedod watch from the shore, Sam wades into the water to take a closer look . . . "We're in luck!" he calls as he manages to right the overturned boat. "She's hardly been damaged at all. The mast is intact and the rudder's all right too!" "Fancy surviving that storm!" marvels Odmedod. "Yes," says Rupert. "I was sure she'd be dashed to pieces on the rocks. When we swam ashore, she must have floated free, then drifted into the sheltered waters of the bay . . ."

Pulling the Venture into shallow water, Sam starts to bail her out. "It will be a while before we're ready," he tells the pals. "Why don't you have a last look round before we set sail?" "Come with us!" cry the cockatoos. "We don't get many visitors and there's plenty here to see . . ." "Where are we going?" asks Odmedod. "To get a souvenir!" calls one of the cockatoos. "You ought to have something to show for your trip. It's not every day a scarecrow puts to sea . . ."

RUPERT DISCOVERS A HIDDEN CAVE

A narrow cave mouth – in they fly.
"Come on!" they call. "This way!" But why?

A hidden marvel greets the pair
As crystals sparkle everywhere!

The cave is full of rare shells too.
"Why don't you take one home with you?"

"Thanks!" Rupert says. "You're kind to show
Us round, but now we have to go!"

Hurrying after the cockatoos, Rupert and Odmedod come to a narrow cave mouth at the foot of the cliffs. The birds fly inside and call to the pals to follow. At first it looks dark and gloomy, but as they venture forward the pair find themselves in a large cavern full of beautiful crystals. The walls glint and shimmer with rainbow colours, while the sea washes into a sparkling pool. "Goodness!" blinks Rupert. "What a surprise! We'd never have found it without the cockatoos . . ."

The crystal cave is a wonderful discovery, but Odmedod can't see any sign of the souvenir the cockatoos promised him. "Look by the pool!" they call. Odmedod clambers to the back of the cave and gasps with surprise. "Shells!" he cries delightedly. "Look, Rupert! They're all different colours . . ." "What better souvenir of your visit?" smile the cockatoos. "Thank you," beam the chums. "We'd better start back now," says Rupert. "We don't want to keep Sam waiting . . ."

RUPERT SAILS HOME

Sam waves, then calls, "Come on, you two!
The Venture's waiting for her crew!"

The swallow joins them as they start.
"I'll guide you as you've lost your chart!"

"Thank you!" calls Sam. "I know the way
From here. Enjoy your holiday!"

The pals spot land. It's nearly night.
At last their journey's end's in sight!

"Come on!" calls Sam as Rupert and Odmedod hurry back. "We're ship-shape and ready to sail…" The only thing Sam hasn't been able to save are his charts and maps, which were completely ruined by the sea. "Never mind!" chirps the swallow. "I'll show you the way. We birds don't need any maps!" Bidding farewell to the cockatoos, the two chums clamber aboard the Venture which is soon underway, with her sails billowing as they follow the swallow out to sea …

The swallow flies on ahead until Sam reaches more familiar waters. "Thanks for your help," cries the sailor. "I can find my way back from here!" "Goodbye!" call Rupert and Odmedod, waving up to the little bird. "Safe journey!" it trills. "I'm going South again now, but I'll see you in Nutwood when summer arrives …" Before long the pals can see white cliffs gleaming on the horizon. "England!" cheers Sam. "We'll soon be back in harbour …"

*Sam furls the Venture's sails and then
Speeds back to Nutwood once again.*

*"Home!" Odmedod smiles. "Life at sea
Was thrilling! Thanks for taking me!"*

*At Rupert's house the happy pair
Recount their voyage to Mrs. Bear.*

*"I've such a lot of things to tell.
We lost our way, but found a shell!"*

In no time at all, the pals are speeding through the night, tucked up in Sam's sidecar. "I never thought I'd be so glad to see dry land!" he declares. When they reach Nutwood, the first thing they do is take Odmedod back to the farm. "Thank you for a wonderful holiday," he smiles. "Glad you enjoyed it!" laughs Sam. "After all you've been through, you can call yourself a regular sea dog!" "Perhaps," nods the scarecrow, "but from now on I'll stick to my fields . . ."

Mrs. Bear is waiting up for Rupert when he finally returns home with Sam. "Hello!" she smiles. "Did you have a nice time?" "Yes, thanks!" cries Rupert. "We saw the cockatoos' crystal cave!" "Cockatoos?" blinks Mr. Bear as he hears Rupert's tale. "Look at the shell they gave me!" smiles Rupert. "Did your friend enjoy the trip too?" asks Mrs. Bear. "Oh yes," laughs Rupert. "But I think he's even happier to be safely back in Nutwood . . ."

THE END

RUPERT and the

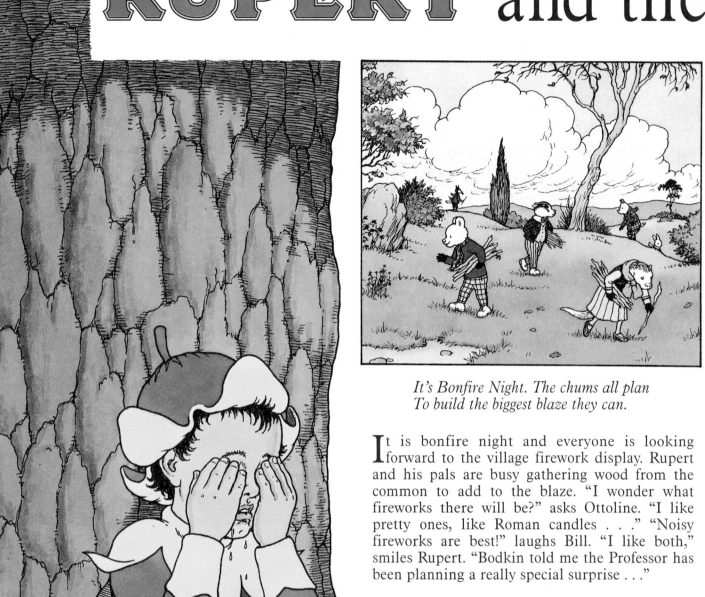

*It's Bonfire Night. The chums all plan
To build the biggest blaze they can.*

It is bonfire night and everyone is looking forward to the village firework display. Rupert and his pals are busy gathering wood from the common to add to the blaze. "I wonder what fireworks there will be?" asks Ottoline. "I like pretty ones, like Roman candles . . ." "Noisy fireworks are best!" laughs Bill. "I like both," smiles Rupert. "Bodkin told me the Professor has been planning a really special surprise . . ."

Noisy Firework

"What fireworks do you think there'll be?"
"Some noisy ones!" cries Bill with glee.

The old Professor's there to show
Where all the sticks they've found should go.

"Well done!" cries the Professor when he sees how much wood the pals have gathered. "Bodkin can use that to finish building the fire . . ." Handing in their bundles, the chums hurry home for tea, promising to meet up later, as soon as it gets dark. Quite a crowd has gathered by the time the Bears arrive and Rupert can see the Professor waiting to light the fire. "Not long until the fireworks start!" declares Mr. Bear.

That evening, Bill and Rupert run
To join the others in the fun.

RUPERT ENJOYS THE FIREWORKS

The bonfire blazes; rockets fly
And showers of bright stars fill the sky.

"Look!" Rupert hears his pal, Bill, yell.
"A noisy rocket! I can tell . . ."

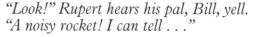

The rocket shoots up overhead,
Then changes colour – blue to red!

It ends up with a bang so loud
It deafens the astonished crowd!

When everyone is gathered round, the Professor lights the bonfire and calls for Bodkin to begin the display. A mighty rocket shoots up into the sky, exploding in a mass of golden stars. "Beautiful!" sighs Ottoline. "Bravo!" cheers Mr. Bear. As Rupert looks on the Professor sets off coloured flares, crackling cascades and a humming saucer. The great bonfire flares up in a tremendous blaze and everyone basks in its glow. "Now for the big surprise!" whispers Bill.

No sooner has Bill spoken than a huge rocket takes off in a streak of silver. Up and up it rises, until it is almost lost from sight. "Gosh!" says Rupert. "It's the biggest firework I've every seen . . .' Next moment, the rocket explodes in a series of deafening bangs, filling the sky with rainbow-coloured spangles. "Crikey!" gasps Bill. "I thought you liked noise?" laughs Rupert. "What a din!" complains Ottoline. "I'm glad the others weren't like that!"

RUPERT MEETS HORACE HEDGEHOG

"My fault!" the old Professor beams.
"I overdid the noise, it seems!"

As everyone is homeward bound
The pals hear a strange rustling sound . . .

It's Horace Hedgehog – wide awake.
"The noise those dreadful fireworks make!"

"I'm meant to hibernate! but how
Can folk sleep with that awful row?"

"I say!" laughs the Professor. "Rather overdid it with that last rocket, I'm afraid! I'd no idea it would be so noisy . . ." Now that the fireworks are over, everyone begins to make their way home. While Mr. and Mrs. Bear lead the way, Rupert and Bill stop for a final glance at the bonfire. As the pair set off across the common they hear a sudden rustling in a nearby pile of leaves. "What's that?" gasps Bill. "I don't know," says Rupert. "But there's definitely someone there . . ."

As Rupert gets closer, the rustling grows more agitated and a grumpy-looking hedgehog emerges from under the leaves. "Horace!" he cries. "What are you doing here, and why are you wearing a nightcap?" "I'm trying to sleep!" complains Rupert's friend. "Hedgehogs hibernate in the winter, you know. I'd just settled down for a nice long nap when lots of bangs and crashes woke me up . . ." "Oh, dear!" says Rupert. "That must have been the firework display."

"Oh, dear!" says Bill. "I'd no idea
That creatures underground could hear!"

The pals apologise and then
The hedgehog disappears again.

Next morning Rupert's chums call by.
"We're off to play football!" they cry.

The Professor explains that they
Must play their game further away . . .

"Don't be cross," says Bill. "We didn't mean to wake you up. I didn't know you could hear fireworks underground! We'll ask the Professor to make them quieter for next year's display . . ." "Good!" says Horace. "Now that they've finished, perhaps I can get back to sleep . . ." "Come on, you two!" calls Mr. Bear, looking to see where the pals have got to. Rupert turns to wave to Horace but the hedgehog has already disappeared, back to his leafy home.

Next morning Rupert and his pals decide to play football together on the common. "Weren't the fireworks good?" says Rupert. "Yes", agrees Willie. "What a display!" When they reach the common, the chums find the Professor and Bodkin clearing up after last night's fire. "Keep well away!" warns the Professor as Bodkin rakes up the smouldering embers. "Fires can be dangerous, even when they've nearly gone out!" The pals agree to go and play on the far side of the common.

70

RUPERT SPOTS SOME DAFFODILS

"Goal!" Willie cries, but then, instead,
The ball sails over Rupert's head . . .

As Rupert gets the ball he blinks.
"A daffodil! How odd!" he thinks.

"More daffodils! But why and how?
They grow in early Spring, not now!"

"I'll take a bunch back home to show
My parents. Perhaps they might know . . ."

The pals are soon enjoying a lively game, with Rupert taking a turn in goal. "Too high!" he calls as Willie kicks the ball over his head. "Sorry!" cries the little mouse. Rupert runs to get the ball, which has landed behind a clump of bushes. As he bends to pick it up, he suddenly stops and blinks in amazement. "A daffodil!" he gasps. "What's that doing here? I didn't know daffodils grew in November. I've only seen them in the Spring, when the weather's much milder . . ."

Rupert is about to go back with the football when he suddenly spots a second clump of daffodils, not far from the first. "Look what I've found!" he calls to the others. "Daffodils!" gasps Willie. "They shouldn't be out at this time of year. It's too cold for flowers. The first sign of frost will finish them off . . ." The chums resume their game of football, but as soon as it ends Rupert decides to pick some daffodils and take them home to show his parents . . .

RUPERT FINDS MORE FLOWERS

*"What lovely daffodils! But where
Did you find them?" gasps Mrs. Bear.*

*The flowers leave Mr. Bear amazed.
"Perhaps some the Professor's raised?"*

*Next morning Rupert hurries out
To see if more flowers are about . . .*

*"Yes! Tulips too! More over there –
There seem to be bulbs everywhere!"*

Mrs. Bear is astonished to see Rupert carrying a bunch of yellow daffodils. "My favourites!" she cries. "But where did you get them?" When she hears how he found them growing on the common, Rupert's mother shakes her head in disbelief. "I've never heard of such a thing!" she exclaims. Mr. Bear is puzzled by the daffodils too. "Perhaps they're a special type?" he suggests. "It might be one of the Professor's experiments. But why should he plant them up on the common?"

Next day, as soon as he has finished lunch, Rupert decides to go to see if there are any more daffodils growing on the common. He hurries back to the spot where the chums were playing football and searches carefully all around. At first the common seems bare, then he suddenly spots a clump of bright red tulips. "There are more, over there!" he marvels. "It looks like a trail of spring bulbs leading over the hill . . ." Excitedly, he runs forward to see where it leads.

RUPERT DISCOVERS AN IMP

"A trail! It leads towards that tree . . ."
Thinks Rupert, looking carefully.

But then he hears a crying sound –
It's one of Nutwood's Imps he's found!

The Imp jumps up and runs away.
"Wait!" Rupert calls. "I'll help you. Stay!"

"I thought Spring was your time of year?"
"It is – but I've been stranded here!"

Following the trail of flowers across the common, Rupert finally comes to a large old oak tree. As he gets nearer, he can hear the sound of somebody crying. "I wonder what's wrong?" he thinks and creeps forward to see who is there. To Rupert's surprise, it isn't one of his chums he can hear, but a small figure, dressed in colourful clothes and a pointed hat. "An Imp of Spring!" he murmurs. "But what's an Imp doing here in the middle of winter? and why is he so upset?"

As Rupert steps forward, the little Imp gives a cry of alarm and jumps to his feet. "Hello!" smiles Rupert. "Don't be afraid. I've only come to see what's wrong . . ." "Everything!" sobs the Imp. "It's cold and damp and not at all like Spring. I ought to be tucked up in a nice warm bed . . ." "I know!" says Rupert. "I thought you all stayed underground until Winter ended?" "We do!" sniffs the miserable Imp. "I came out early to look at something and now I can't get back . . ."

RUPERT HEARS THE IMP'S TALE

The Imp was sleeping underground,
When suddenly, he heard a sound . . .

"I didn't know what it could be
So dressed and came outside to see . . ."

"The coloured lights I saw were so
Enchanting that I couldn't go!"

"At last I hurried home once more
But found a wind had shut the door!"

"It all started when a noisy bang woke me up," explains the Imp. "Everyone else was still sound asleep but I thought I'd go and see what was happening. It was dark when I stepped outside, the sky was full of flashing lights, and a crowd had gathered on the far side of the common." "The Fireworks!" says Rupert. "So that's what they're called!" cries the Imp. "They were so pretty I decided to stay and watch. I couldn't resist leaving the tree and having a closer look . . ."

The Imp tells Rupert that he saw everyone gathered together round a great big fire. "It was cold on the common," he explains, "so I came as close as I could to try and keep warm. As soon as the fireworks ended I hurried back to the hollow tree, only to find that the door had blown shut! I couldn't get it open again, no matter how I tried. The others are all sleeping, so no-one can let me in. It's too chilly to stay out any longer, but I just don't know what else to do . . ."

RUPERT TAKES THE IMP HOME

*"I can't undo the hidden lock
And nobody will hear us knock!"*

*"It's far too cold for you to stay
Out here! Come back with me. This way . . ."*

*"Poor thing!" says Mrs. Bear. "Eat these!
And stay for as long as you please."*

*They put the Imp to bed. "Good night!
We'll talk tomorrow, when it's light."*

Rupert tries knocking at the door in the tree but receives no reply . . . "Are there other entrances to Imp Headquarters?" he asks. "Yes," says the Imp. "But everything's been shut up for the Winter!" "You can't stay out here in the cold!" says Rupert. "Why don't you come home with me?" Wrapping the shivering Imp in his scarf, he leads the way across the common towards the lights of Nutwood. "That's my house," he smiles. "Come in and warm up while we work out what to do next . . ."

Mrs. Bear is amazed to see the little Imp. "I expect you're hungry!" she says when she hears what has happened. "I hope Imps like chocolate biscuits . . ." As they chat by the fire, the Imp tells Rupert that his name is Willow. "I've never been in a house before!" he smiles. "Time you were off to sleep now," says Rupert's mother. "You must be very tired." "Goodnight!" waves Rupert as the Imp settles down. "Tomorrow we'll find a way back to your home . . ."

RUPERT KNOWS THE ANSWER

Next morning, Rupert says that he
Knows someone they should go and see . . .

The Imp thanks Mrs. Bear, then they
Set off together, straightaway.

"It's Horace! He'll know what to do!
He hibernates in winter too . . ."

The hedgehog's fast asleep as well.
"I hope that he can hear the bell!"

Next morning Willow has his first taste of toast and marmalade as he joins the Bears for breakfast. "It's very kind of you to look after me," he smiles, "but I can't stay here all Winter!" "There must be another way back to Imp Headquarters," declares Rupert, then suddenly he has a good idea. "I know somebody we can ask to help us!" he cries. "We'll go and see them as soon as you've finished . . ." "Good luck!" calls Mrs. Bear as the pair set off towards the common.

"Who are we going to see?" asks Willow. "Horace Hedgehog!" laughs Rupert. "He lives underground too . . ." Explaining how Horace was woken by the noise of the fireworks, Rupert pushes aside a pile of old leaves and squeezes through a gap in the tree's roots. Scrambling down a flight of steps, he finds a small wooden door with a bell-pull outside. "Do you think he'll hear?" asks Willow. "I don't know," says Rupert. "Let's hope he doesn't sleep too heavily . . ."

RUPERT VISITS HORACE

The door swings open slowly, then
Horace groans, "No! Not you again . . ."

"I'm sorry!" Rupert says. "But we
Need help! It's an emergency . . ."

As soon as Horace hears what's wrong
He says he'll help. "It won't take long!"

He sets off down a corridor
The Imp has never seen before.

For a long time nothing happens, then Rupert hears the door start to open . . . "Who's there?" calls Horace. "You again!" he gasps. "What do you mean by waking me up for a second time?" "I'm sorry," says Rupert, "but my friend's in trouble and you're the only one who might be able to help . . ." "An Imp!" blinks the hedgehog. "What's he doing out at this time of year? He ought to be in bed!" "That's what's wrong," says Rupert and quickly explains how Willow was stranded . . .

When Horace hears Willow's story, he soon agrees to help the Imp. "We must have both been woken by the same rocket!" he smiles. "You were right to come and see me, Rupert. I *do* know an entrance to Imp Headquarters, although it's hardly ever used." Telling the pair to follow him closely, Horace sets off along a gloomy corridor that passes by his leafy winter chambers. "I'm afraid it's rather narrow at first," he tells Rupert. "But you'll soon be able to stand up properly . . ."

Rupert and the Noisy Firework

RUPERT FOLLOWS THE IMP

"It leads out to a path I share
With Elves and Imps," he tells the pair.

"That's marvellous!" the lost Imp cries.
"This tunnel's one I recognise!"

"Look! There's a sign!" He cries with glee.
"This way, Rupert! Just follow me . . ."

Another sign. The Imps' H.Q.
"We have to go through this door too!"

At the far end of the corridor, Horace unlocks another door to reveal a well-lit passageway. "You should recognise where you are now," he tells Willow. Sure enough, the little Imp gives a cry of delight as he steps out into the light. "It's one of our main paths!" he laughs. "I've often been this way, but I never knew anyone else lived here!" "Off you go," smiles Horace. "I'm going back to bed now and this time I'm not getting up until Spring has arrived . . ."

Willow is so pleased to be back underground that he scampers along, leaving Rupert far behind. "Wait for me!" he calls, hurrying to catch up. "Sorry!" laughs the Imp. "There isn't much further to go now. All we have to do is follow the signs . . ." "Do you ever get lost?" asks Rupert. "Sometimes," admits Willow. "The best thing then is to pop up and have a look above ground." Reaching another door, he pushes it open and beckons for Rupert to follow . . .

RUPERT SEES A DORMITORY

"Quiet now!" the Imp warns. "Not a peep!
"The others should be fast asleep . . ."

"Thank goodness! No-one saw me go.
Now nobody need ever know!"

The Imp yawns as he dons his cap.
"Now I'll resume my winter nap!"

He thanks Rupert and then declares.
"The way home's up that flight of stairs!"

As they enter Imp Headquarters, Rupert notices the lights growing dimmer. "We're nearly at the Dormitory now," whispers Willow. "Try not to make any noise . . ." He pulls aside a heavy curtain and Rupert hears a gentle snoring sound coming from within. Creeping forward he sees a long room lined with hundreds of beds, each of which contains a peacefully-slumbering Imp. "No-one else is awake!" says Willow. "With a bit of luck, they'll never know I've been outside . , ."

Now that he is back in the Dormitory, Willow soon feels drowsy. "I'm glad I saw the fireworks," he yawns, "but there's nothing I'd like better than a nice long nap . . ." "Perhaps you can visit us again when Winter's over? " says Rupert. "You'll always be welcome to come to tea . . ." "Thank you," says the Imp. "And thanks for all your help!" Out in the corridor, he points to a steep flight of steps. "That's the way to Nutwood," he smiles. "Just keep climbing up . . ."

RUPERT RETURNS

The winding staircase seems to stop
Abruptly as he nears the top!

Then, opening a little door,
He finds himself outside once more . . .

Nearby stand Bill and Ottoline.
They've no idea where Rupert's been!

"What lovely blooms!" Ottoline cries.
"The last till Spring!" Rupert replies.

Waving goodbye to his new friend, Rupert clambers up the winding staircase. Before long, he finds himself surrounded by a tangle of roots, which gets thicker and thicker the further he goes. At last he reaches what seems to be a dead-end. "It must be a door!" he thinks and pushes against it with all his might. Suddenly, he finds himself back on Nutwood common, where he first met Willow. "If only the others were here," he smiles. "Imagine how surprised they'd be!"

No sooner has Rupert closed the door in the tree than he spots Ottoline and Bill, following the trail of tulips and daffodils. "Hello!" calls Ottoline. "Aren't these flowers lovely!" "Rupert found them yesterday," laughs Bill, "when we were out playing football . . ." "Are there any more?" she asks. "No!" smiles Rupert, thinking of the sleeping Imps. "I'm sure that's the last of them. We won't see any more daffodils now until the start of Spring . . ."

THE END

RUPERT'S
ANNIVERSARY COLOURING COMPETITION

HUNDREDS OF POUNDS IN PRIZES!

RUPERT'S Colouring Competition is open to all readers up to the age of 10 on 31st January 1996, and is free to enter. Every boy and girl – even the youngest – will have a chance of winning one of the splendid money prizes, so try your very best when you colour the Competition picture, which is on the next page. Read the rules carefully and be sure to get your entry to us before the closing date, 31st January, 1996.

How the Prizes will be Awarded

Entries will be divided into three groups

GROUP 1 ... up to 4 years
GROUP 2 ... 5-7 years
GROUP 3 ... 8-10 years

In each of the three groups the following prizes will be awarded

1st £100
2nd £50
3rd £30
4th £20

All prizes will be forwarded not later than 31st March, 1996. A list of prize-winners will be sent on application to Rupert's Colouring Competition, Pedigree Books Limited, The Old Rectory, Matford Lane, Exeter, EX2 4PS.

Rules of the Competition

1. Colour the picture as nicely as you can with paints, colouring pencils, crayons, or felt tip pen.

2. Age, skill and neatness will be taken into consideration.

3. Complete the entry form with your age, name and address. Do not detach the form from the picture. A parent, guardian or teacher must certify that the colouring is entirely your own work.

4. Send your picture together with the entry form in a sealed envelope to RUPERT'S COLOURING COMPETITION, Pedigree Books Limited, The Old Rectory, Matford Lane, Exeter, EX2 4PS.

5. All entries must be received on or before 31st January, 1996. No entry will be accepted after this date.

6. Children of employees of Pedigree Books are not allowed to enter.

7. The judges' decision is final and no correspondence will be allowed. Unfortunately no entries can be returned.

8. The competition is open to UK residents only.

9. Only one entry is allowed per person.

THE PICTURE TO COLOUR IS ON THE NEXT PAGE

RUPERT'S COLOURING COMPETITION

These two pictures of Rupert looking through his telescope look identical, but there are ten differences between them. Can you spot them all?
Answers on page 97

S P O T   T H E   D I F F E R E N C E

See how many of Rupert's friends you can recognise, you can find the answers on page 86

The first story about Rupert, the little bear who lives in Nutwood, began in the Daily Express on 8th November 1920. His many subsequent adventures have appeared continuously in the newspaper ever since, and in 1936 these stories started to be reproduced in the Rupert Annual. Rupert's sixty-fifth anniversary and the publication of the fiftieth edition of the annual coincided in 1985. To mark the occasion, the cover of that book, painted by John Harrold, contained more of the characters who have shared – and still share – Rupert's adventures than have ever previously appeared in one illustration. As a tribute to his famous predecessor, the great Rupert storyteller/artist Alfred Bestall MBE, John Harrold included him in the picture. A print of the painting can be seen on the previous pages.

KEY TO THE CHARACTERS

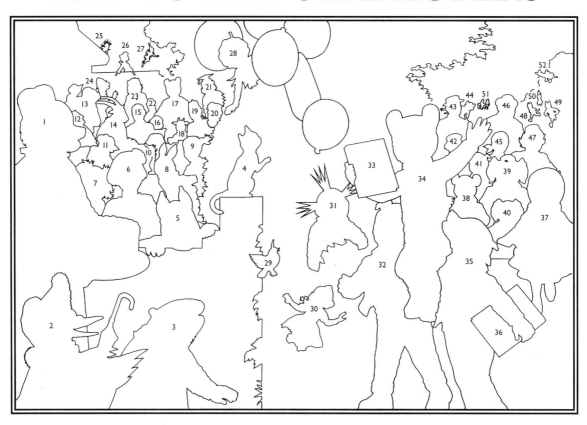

1 Mrs. Bear, his mother.
2 Lily Duckling, a timid friend.
3 Gregory Guineapig, a young, sometimes silly, friend.
4 Dinkie, a mischievous cat.
5 Podgy Pig, a greedy but goodhearted friend.
6 Tigerlily, the Chinese Conjurer's daughter.
7 Pong-Ping who came to Nutwood from China.
8 Rich Reggie Rabbit – or is it Rex? It's one of the twins.
9 Sara, a friend from Nutwood village.
10 Pong-Ping's pet dragon, Ming.
11 Rastus, the country mouse.
12 The Gipsy Granny, an old friend.
13 Gaffer Jarge, Nutwood's oldest inhabitant.
14 The Wise Old Goat. Friendly but a bit mysterious.
15 Alfred Bestall MBE who wrote and drew the adventures of Rupert for over thirty years.
16 Margot, a little girl Rupert has known for as long as he can remember.
17 Mr. Bear, his father.
18 Billy Goat, the Wise Old Goat's nephew.
19 The Chinese Conjurer, a magician.
20 Captain Binnacle, an old seafaring friend.
21 Dr. Chimp, Nutwood's schoolmaster.
22 Beryl, one of three Nutwood Girl Guides (the others are Janet and Pauline) and owner of Dinkie.
23 Dr. Lion, Nutwood's doctor.
24 Constable Growler, village bobby.
25 An Autumn Elf. The Elves ensure that trees and growing things can rest after the summer.
26 Odmedod, a scarecrow who can talk to Rupert.

27 Jack Frost, bringer of snow and ice to Nutwood.
28 An Imp of Spring. The Imps waken everything that has slept through the winter.
29 A Nutwood Robin. When the local robins were turned yellow Rupert restored their colour for them.
30 Dutch Doll who refused to be put down the chimney with Santa Claus's other toys.
31 Chinese Doll, Rupert's guide to the Land of Games.
32 Algy Pug, a very close chum.
33 The First Rupert Annual (1936).
34 The little bear himself.
35 Bill Badger, another very close friend.
36 The Fiftieth Rupert Annual.
37 Rosalie, Podgy Pig's tiresome cousin.
38 Willie Mouse, an old friend.
39 Edward Trunk, another close chum.
40 Pompey, Edward's baby brother.
41 Bingo, a brainy friend.
42 Margaret, a friend.
43 Sailor Sam, a close friend ever since they shared an Arctic adventure.
44 Beppo, a bundle of mischief.
45 Rollo, a friend, grandson of the Gipsy Granny.
46 The Old Professor, a friendly inventor.
47 The Professor's servant.
48 Ferdy Fox, usually up to no good.
49 His brother Freddy.
50 Ting-Ling, a young Chinese visitor.
51 Two of Nutwood's Scouts.
52 Santa Claus's cowboy messenger.

Rupert's Memory Test

How good is your memory? How carefully have you read all Rupert's adventures in the annual? Find out now by studying the pictures below. Each is part of a bigger picture you will have seen in a story. When you have had a good look at them, try to answer the questions at the bottom of the page. Then check the stories to discover if you were right. *Answers on page 97*

CAN YOU REMEMBER . . .

1. Who is Rupert visiting?
2. Why is Rupert frightened?
3. Who has knocked Rupert over?
4. What has the professor invented?
5. What is the horse's name and to whom does he belong?
6. What are Rupert and his father trying to buy?
7. Who is Rupert running to see and why?
8. What is Captain Binnacle showing Rupert and what does it do?
9. What has Rupert got and how did he come to get it?
10. What constellation is the missing star from?
11. Who is Rupert looking for?
12. What woke Horace up?
13. Why are the pals getting a picnic?
14. Who owns the forest and why is he cross?
15. What is Rupert doing and why?
16. Who is crying and why?

WORD SEARCH

Jumbled up below are the names of the eight characters surrounding the puzzle.
You will have to look closely as the names may read diagonally,
or from right to left, left to right or top to bottom.

If you get stuck, the answers can be found on page 97.

```
A V M N B U O A J L H F V G W U
A T D E Q I Z F M A Q W E R I K
C H X J L S L O A S D F G H L J
A P A S F C M L Y L K J H G F D
P K B I L A E T B Z V B N M C X
T U W Q T H C Z M A I J A Z K F
A M H O R A C E H E D G E H O G
I D F L U Z Q R T Y B G U I O A
N A Z C S B G H J O R U E O D B
B S F D T G J Y T P Q B I R M V
I O W I L A R M U E R T B I E D
N F D A L G Y P U G E S W S D U
N M O K T S Y U S E B M Z I O L
A W I M I L C A P A I V R E D O
C R N G I N R A E B T R E P U R
L E N B L O K I J U H Y G T F W
E P O M U N T B R C E W X I U B
N O N V W I L L I E M O U S E G
```

MAKE A CHRISTMAS TREE
JUST LIKE RUPERT'S

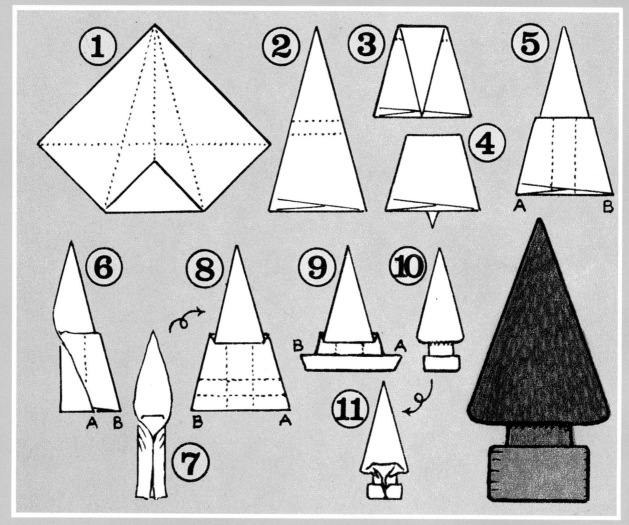

You will need a square of thin paper. Fold opposite corners together each way to find the middle and fold one corner part way to the centre (Fig. 1). Fold both sides in along the sloping dotted lines (Fig. 2), note the new dotted lines and bring the top point to the middle of the bottom edge to give the upper crease (Fig. 3) and then fold the point backwards using the other dotted line (Fig 4). Bring the point up again keeping both folds pressed (Fig. 5) and mark two upright lines, as shown, at equal distances from the corners A and B. Take A across to a spot on the bottom edge that will make a fold at the lefthand dotted line. Press that fold only as far up as the middle crease (Fig. 6) and do the same to B so that A and B can be held forward together (Fig. 7). Separate A and B as in Fig. 5 and turn the paper over (Fig. 8). Fold the bottom edge up, then over again, following the horizontal dotted lines (Fig. 9). Take B and A round to the back and the creases of Figs. 6 and 7 will cause the Christmas tree (Fig. 10) to take shape. Turn it over again (Fig. 11), lock the end of B into A, then gently flatten the folds at the back into the form required. If the 'tub' is slightly rounded the tree will stand up.

(This version of his Christmas tree was sent to Rupert by Mr. Robert Harbin, the Origami man.)

HOW TO MAKE
RUPERT'S TOY CAMERA

This toy will give you lots of fun.

(You may need to ask an adult to help you with the scissors.) First cut a piece of thin springy card to the same size as the pattern on the right. Trace the shaped top piece on to your card, then cut it out.

Next use a ruler to mark out the two inner panels, drawing dotted lines on three sides of each. Carefully cut round the dotted lines leaving the fourth side uncut to make two flaps. Stick a "photo" on the upper flap. If you do not wish to cut up your annual, you can draw one yourself or take one from a magazine.

Fold back the card along the centre line so that the lower flap is behind the one with the picture on it (fig.1). At this stage colour your camera as in fig. 1, and finish it off by gumming on a thin slice of cork as a "lens" and a scrap of cellophane as a "view-finder."

Now push back the picture flap and at the same time bring the red flap forward (fig. 2) so that it covers the picture altogether as in fig. 3. Your camera is now ready. Hold the folded card at the top edges, then open them smartly, like a book. As you do so the red flap will slip back and the picture flap will appear – just as though you had taken a photograph!

FOLD ALONG THIS LINE

① CELLOPHANE

THIN SLICE OF CORK

②

③

RUPERT'S MAZE OF BUTTERFLIES

Start at the flower in the top left-hand corner and trace your way along the white paths until you reach the flower in the bottom right-hand corner. Only one of the paths will lead you there . . . the others are put in to puzzle you. When you have found the right path, hold the page at arm's length and you will soon see the shape of another butterfly in the white lines. You can then have the fun of shading the outline with your pencil to make the butterfly stand out boldly.

RUPERT'S BUTTERFLY PUZZLE

You will find that the pattern of the butterfly's wings is made up of parts of the coloured scene. Start with the left-hand wing and copy the colour of each piece. Remember that some of the shapes are turned a different way, but this will add to the fun of finding them. The colours of the right-hand wing can be copied from the opposite one.

Your Own Rupert Story

Title: _____

Why not try colouring the pictures below and writing a story to fit them?
Write your story in four parts, one for each picture, saying what it shows.
Then, faintly in pencil, print each part neatly on the lines under its
picture. When they fit, go over the printing with a pen. There is space
at the top for a title.

_____   _____
_____   _____
_____   _____

_____   _____
_____   _____
_____   _____

Copy Colour

Here's Rupert and some of his friends;
can you copy the colours onto the opposite page?

Copy Colour

Colour in the pictures below

DOT TO DOT

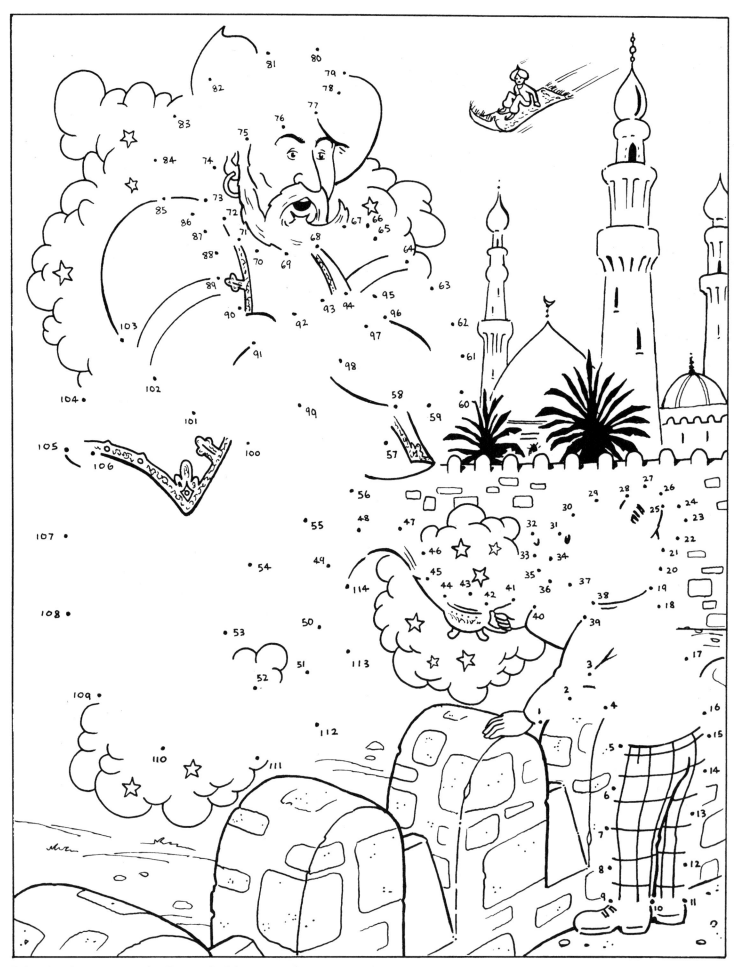

Join the dots to see who Rupert's friend is . . .

ANSWERS

MEMORY TEST

1. Horace Hedgehog
2. The Venture has been caught in a storm
3. Dr. Watson
4. A special tree tonic to stop the pine needles from falling
5. Pegasus belongs to Stella
6. A Christmas tree
7. Horace Hedgehog as he knows an entrance to Imp Headquarters
8. A sextant used by sailors to navigate at sea by the stars
9. A shell he got from the crystal cave as a souvenir from the cockatoos
10. The Seven Sisters
11. His friend Odmedod
12. A noisy firework
13. For helping Farmer Brown gather the hay
14. The Pine King and he's cross because Rupert and Bodkin are digging up one of his pine trees
15. Rupert is sprinkling luminous powder on the floor to catch the thief by following his footprints
16. An Imp of Spring – he's crying because he left the Imp Headquarters to watch the fireworks that woke him up, but he can't get back in

A	V	M	N	B	U	O	A	J	L	H	F	V	G	W	U
A	T	D	E	Q	I	Z	F	M	A	Q	W	E	R	I	K
C	H	X	J	L	S	L	O	A	S	D	F	G	H	L	J
A	P	A	S	F	C	M	L	Y	L	K	J	H	G	F	D
P	K	B	I	L	A	E	T	B	Z	V	B	N	M	C	X
T	U	W	Q	T	H	C	Z	M	A	I	J	A	Z	K	F
A	M	H	O	R	A	C	E	H	E	D	G	E	H	O	G
I	D	F	L	U	Z	Q	R	T	Y	B	G	U	I	O	A
N	A	Z	C	S	B	G	H	J	O	R	U	E	O	D	B
B	S	F	D	T	G	J	Y	T	P	Q	B	I	R	M	V
I	O	W	I	L	A	R	M	U	E	R	T	B	I	E	D
N	F	D	A	L	G	Y	P	U	G	E	S	W	S	D	U
N	M	O	K	T	S	Y	U	S	E	B	M	Z	I	O	L
A	W	I	M	I	L	C	A	P	A	I	V	R	E	D	O
C	R	N	G	I	N	R	A	E	B	T	R	E	P	U	R
L	E	N	B	L	O	K	I	J	U	H	Y	G	T	F	W
E	P	O	M	U	N	T	B	R	C	E	W	X	I	U	B
N	O	N	V	W	I	L	L	I	E	M	O	U	S	E	G

RUPERT and the

"Hello!" calls Rupert eagerly.
"We're off to buy a Christmas tree!"

It is a snowy December morning and Rupert and Mr. Bear are on their way to buy a Christmas tree. As they walk along the High Street, Rupert spots some of his chums, peering in the window of the toy shop. "Hello!" calls Bill. "Not long to wait for Christmas now!" When they reach the greengrocer's Mr. Bear stops with a gasp. "Dear me!" he cries. "They haven't got a single tree left! Let's go in and see what's wrong . . ."

Christmas Tree

But when they reach the shop, the pair
Soon learn that there are no trees there!

"I'm sorry! They're in short supply.
The forest's sick. I don't know why!"

"Sorry!" says Mr. Chimp. "I normally order lots of trees for Christmas, but this year there just aren't any to be found. Something's wrong with the forest and none of the pine or spruce are good enough to use!" "What a shame!" says Rupert. "It won't be the same without a tree . . ." As the pair leave the shop someone else is reading the dismal sign. "Bodkin!" says Rupert. "He must have come to buy a tree for the Professor . . ."

Outside the grocer's Rupert sees
Bodkin reading about the trees . . .

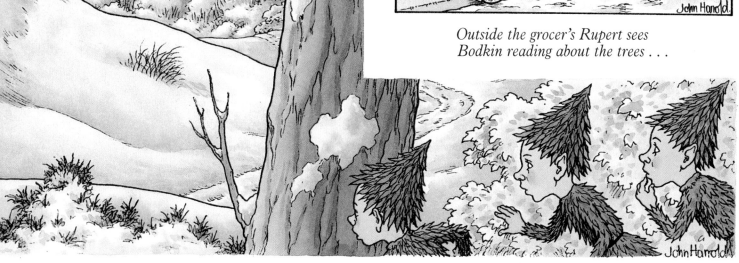

RUPERT SHARES A PROBLEM

*"None left!" he gasps. "But I've been sent.
For one for an experiment . . ."*

*"I'd better go and see what's wrong.
Perhaps you'd like to come along?"*

*"One tree's enough!" calls Mr. Bear.
"We'll put it in the village square!"*

*The old Professor's shocked to find
He can't buy trees of any kind!*

"No trees!" cries the Professor's servant. "I don't believe it . . ." When he hears what's wrong, Bodkin explains that his master needs a Christmas tree for his latest experiment. "He's invented a potion to stop the needles falling off. If I can't find a tree, then how will we ever know if it works?" Thinking for a moment, he tells Rupert he plans to go to the forest to see what's wrong. "Why don't you come too?" he asks. "If we find a healthy tree you can help me carry it back."

Mr. Bear thinks that going to the forest for a tree is a good idea. "Good luck!" he calls as the pair set out. "If you find a nice one we can put it in the village square . . ." Following Bodkin across the snowy fields, Rupert hurries towards the Professor's tower. "Hello!" blinks his old friend. "This *is* a pleasant surprise! But where's the tree I wanted?" "There aren't any!" shrugs Bodkin. "Goodness!" gasps the Professor. "How odd! Come in and tell me what's happened . . ."

Rupert and the Christmas Tree

RUPERT VISITS THE FOREST

*"I've made a tonic that should stop
Trees letting all their needles drop!"*

*"Come on!" calls Bodkin. "Off we go!
I'll tow you there, across the snow . . ."*

*Beyond the common, Rupert sees
A forest full of tall pine trees.*

*The pines grow side by side, packed tight,
So dense there's hardly any light.*

Leading the way to his laboratory, the Professor shows Rupert the new potion. "It's a special tree tonic!" he explains. "Falling needles should be a thing of the past, although I need to try it out on a Christmas tree before I can be certain!" "Bodkin and I are going into the woods to look for one!" says Rupert excitedly. "He said we'd use a sledge to carry it back . . ." When everything is ready, Bodkin tells Rupert to climb aboard. "Hold tight!" he calls. "We're on our way!"

Swishing across the common, Rupert soon spots the beginning of Nutwood forest. Even the familiar trees look different under a heavy blanket of snow. On the far side of the wood, the pair come to a steep hill, which they whizz down together, with Bodkin riding on the back of the sledge. When their ride ends, they find themselves at the edge of the pine forest. The trees here are tall and close together, while the way ahead looks dark and gloomy . . .

101

RUPERT MEETS THE PINE KING

"This tree looks perfect! Not too big,"
Says Bodkin and prepares to dig . . .

Green spiky woodland Imps appear.
"Our King has banned all digging here!"

The Pine King comes. "What's this I see?
I cannot spare a single tree!"

"The pines are sick! Their needles fall.
Some unknown blight has struck them all!"

Following a narrow track through the trees, Rupert and Bodkin make their way into the silent forest. The tall pines are much too big to take back to Nutwood, but in a clearing they come across a smaller tree that looks ideal. "Perfect!" says Bodkin. "As soon as I've dug it up, you can help me load it aboard." He is about to begin, when the silence of the forest is broken by an angry cry. "Stop!" calls a shrill voice. "The Pine King has forbidden the taking of trees . . ."

To Rupert and Bodkin's astonishment, they find themselves surrounded by an angry group of woodland Imps . . . "We didn't mean any harm," begins Rupert, then breaks off as he spots an imposing figure, wearing a crown of cones. "What's this?" demands the King. "Who dares disturb the silence of Our Realm?" When he hears what Rupert and Bodkin want, he tells them a terrible blight has struck the forest. "The trees are all sickly and shedding their needles!"

RUPERT HAS AN IDEA

"We'd like to save the forest too . . .
If only I knew what to do!"

Then Rupert smiles. "There is a way!
Let's hurry back without delay . . ."

"The old Professor holds the key.
His tonic sounds just right to me!"

The pair explain what's wrong, and how
They hope to save the pine trees now.

"So that's why there are no Christmas trees this year!" gasps Rupert. "Aye!" declares the Pine King. "My guards have strict orders. Until the forest recovers, there can be no trees to spare!" "But that's terrible!" says Rupert. "If only there was something we could do . . ." Then he suddenly has a good idea. "Perhaps we *can* help save the forest after all!" he tells the King. "Come on, Bodkin. Follow me! We've got to get back to Nutwood as quickly as we can . . ."

As they set out for Nutwood, Rupert tells Bodkin what he has in mind. "The Professor's new tonic!" he smiles. "If it can stop trees shedding their needles, then perhaps it can make them better too?" The pair speed back on the sledge, then run breathlessly into the tower to tell the professor everything that has happened. "Dear me!" he cries. "I had no idea the forest was in such a sorry state. I don't know if my mixture will do the trick, but it's certainly worth a try . . ."

"It might help," Rupert's friend agrees.
"We'll spray it on the weakest trees . . ."

"I'll fly above the trees. Your task
Will be to spray them from this flask."

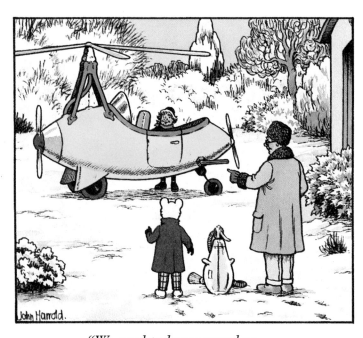

"We need to hover very low
And spray the forest as we go."

They fly to where the pine wood lies.
"Get ready!" the Professor cries.

"We'll have to spray the trees from above!" declares the Professor. "Bodkin can get a flying machine ready, while you help in the laboratory." "Can I fly in the plane too?" asks Rupert. "Of course!" smiles his friend. "You and Bodkin can work the spray together." The Professor pours all the tonic into a large flask, then fixes a long hose to the top. "We haven't got enough to cover the whole forest," he tells Rupert, "so your job is to pick out the most needy-looking trees . . ."

When Rupert and the Professor go outside, they find that Bodkin has already wheeled the flying machine from its hangar. "I'll start the engine!" calls the Professor. "You and Rupert climb aboard and we'll be on our way . . ." In no time at all, the friends are soaring high above the snow-covered fields of Nutwood and on towards the Pine King's forest. "We'll try to hover just above the tree-tops," explains the Professor. "Don't start spraying until I've got as close as I can . . ."

RUPERT SPRAYS THE TREES

"Start now!" he calls out. "Fire away!"
So Rupert starts to aim the spray.

"That's it!" cries Rupert. "One tree done!
Now I'll begin another one . . ."

At last the flask is empty, then
The three fly homeward once again.

"But will it work?" "We'll have to wait!
You'd better go now. Don't be late!"

Circling over the blighted pine forest, the Professor's plane sinks lower and lower, until it is just above the tops of the trees. Steadying the heavy flask, Bodkin starts to pump the handle, while Rupert takes aim with the spray. "Now!" calls the Professor. Bodkin turns a lever and a fine mist drenches the nearest tree. Moving forward, they spray the next pine, then another and another, until Rupert loses count. "Well done!" cries the Professor. "Excellent work!"

Spraying the pine trees takes a long time and it is late afternoon before Rupert's work is done. "We've used every last drop of tonic!" declares Bodkin as his master flies back to Nutwood. "I wonder if the Pine King saw us?" By the time they land, the sky is growing dark and Rupert has to hurry home for tea. "Do you think the trees will get better now?" he asks the Professor. "I hope so," smiles his friend, "but I don't really know. All we can do is wait until tomorrow . . ."

RUPERT'S PLAN WORKS

*Next morning, Rupert wakes to find
The presents Santa's left behind . . .*

*Then Bodkin calls. "I'm off to see
The pine trees. Will you come with me?"*

*"I hope the tonic's done the trick!
The poorly pines might still be sick . . ."*

*"Look!" Bodkin cries. "They're thick and green!
The healthiest I've ever seen!"*

Next morning, Rupert wakes up to find a bulging stocking at the foot of his bed. "Christmas Day!" he cries and peers inside to see what presents Santa has left. After breakfast, there is a knock at the door and Bodkin wishes everyone a happy Christmas. "I've come to ask if Rupert would like to go to the forest," he explains. "We can see if the Professor's tonic has made any difference to the sickly trees . . ." "Good idea!" smiles Mrs. Bear. "But don't be late for Christmas dinner!"

Striding out across the snow-covered common, Bodkin warns Rupert that the Professor isn't sure his tonic will have done the trick. "He only made it for indoor trees," he says. "Pines in a forest might not like it at all . . ." As they reach the edge of the wood he breaks off with a startled cry. "Look at the difference!" he gasps. The pine trees are greener and bushier than Rupert has ever seen them and even the smallest saplings seem to have grown taller. "Wonderful!" he cries.

RUPERT IS REWARDED

*Then, one by one, Pine Imps appear.
"Your magic spray has worked!" they cheer.*

*The King arrives. "You've saved my trees!
There's no trace left of their disease!"*

*Now that the King has trees to spare,
He gives one to the helpful pair.*

*The Imps have a surprise planned too.
"We'll carry the tree back for you!"*

As Rupert and Bodkin stand admiring the trees, they hear a rustling sound nearby. One by one the Pine King's subjects appear, dancing with delight at how the forest has recovered. "Hurray!" calls their leader. "The Pine Wood has been saved, all thanks to you!" "Bravo!" booms a deep voice as the King himself comes to thank Rupert and Bodkin. "We saw you flying over the forest yesterday," he marvels. "Your spray has worked wonders! The pines have never looked so healthy and green!"

"Now that the forest has recovered, there are plenty of trees to spare," smiles the King. "As a sign of Our gratitude, we have chosen one specially for the village of Nutwood!" As he speaks, more Pine Imps appear, carrying a splendid tree. "Hurrah!" cries Rupert. "We *will* have a Christmas tree, after all!" Bidding farewell to the King, Rupert and Bodkin set off home, with the little Imps carrying the tree behind them. "What a sight!" chuckles Bodkin.

RUPERT'S PALS JOIN IN

When Nutwood comes in sight, they go.
"We can't let people see, you know!"

Soon Rupert's chums all run to see
The wonderful new Christmas tree.

They all bring decorations, and
Soon have a special party planned . . .

That evening, everybody comes.
"A fine tree!" Gaffer tells the chums.

When they reach the outskirts of Nutwood, the Pine Imps tell Rupert they dare not come any further for fear of being seen. "Never mind!" he smiles. "I'm sure Bodkin and I can manage from here. Thanks again for such a splendid gift!" Hauling the tree through the snow, the pair soon spot some of Rupert's chums, who come running to help . . . "What a marvellous tree!" gasps Willie. "We're going to put it in the village square," explains Rupert. "Wonderful!" calls Algy.

As soon as the villagers hear about the Christmas tree, they all offer to help decorate it straightaway. "Splendid!" beams the Professor as Bodkin clambers up a ladder. "I think our little tree-spraying experiment was a definite success..." Later that evening, as darkness falls, everyone gathers round the tree to sing carols and wish each other Happy Christmas. "Well done!" Gaffer Jarge tells Rupert. " 'Tis the finest tree I've ever seen!"

THE END

108

Follow Rupert every day

in the
Daily Express

John Harrold.